MISSING MOON

Lost Xentu
~ Book 3 ~

MARIE JUDSON

INDIES UNITED PUBLISHING HOUSE, LLC
P.O. BOX 3071
QUINCY, IL 62305-3071

OTHER BOOKS by MARIE JUDSON

Braided Dimensions Series

Braided Dimensions: Book 1
Stretched Across Time: Book 2
Strange Alliances: Book 3
Pasts Undone: Book 4

Lost Xentu Series

Elf Stone of the Neyna
A Far Cry
Missing Moon

CHAPTER

1

Yanda curled on the rug in the comfortable living space next to the ship control room, tapping keys on her ENAC. She searched on her advanced portable computer for her missing eight-year-old daughter.

Through the open doorway to the control room, Tlalit, female forest elf and captain of the *Sarsefi*, remarked on star systems as they hurtled through space. Yanda could see see the tall female elf with tangerine hair in a peak run ringed and tattooed fingers over panels that blinked lights of myriad colors,

Yanda's son Zami crouched at her feet constructing towers with *plunka* blocks.

"Tell me again what Seiti said to you when you had your vision on that hostile moon." Merne, the captain Tlalit's partner, lay back in a massage unit next to Yanda. On her shoulder, next to her long leaf-shaped ear, a miniature simian native to her elven forest, perched, round eyes staring from under a gold forelock, tail wrapped across her shoulders. When he finished playing with her braids, clipped in an elaborate pattern, he ran across to his other favorite being, Zami, and climbed to his shoulder. The three-year old stroked him with affection and delight.

Yanda pushed back hair streaked of crimson and ebony. "You think I really spoke to Seiti, not some hologram created by an evil abducting mage?"

Vatu, next to her, put a hand on her leg. "Of course you talked to her." Vatu's eyes, with their nictating membranes, sought hers with kindness and concern. A blue Mingalian female with striking cerulean head nubs, she and Yanda had been close since their long captivity together.

Over the time since the Stones had helped her "reach" her daughter, Yanda had grown suspicious that it hadn't been Seiti at all but some trick of the mind orchestrated by one of their many enemies. "After all, it was in Unknown Space. How could she be there?"

Yanda's precocious half-elf son asked, "What is Unknown Space? How do you know about it if it's not known?"

"Good question." She crawled over to nuzzle his ear. "It should be called Unlivable Space. It's called Unknown because they haven't been able to explore it. Ships can't go there. The Dark Matter destroys the engines. And it's unbreathable, for most sentient beings like us."

Merne sat up. "You don't think you were with Seiti? You were sure enough before we headed out on this excursion." She gave Yanda a steady stare, on the verge of challenging.

Yanda turned to her, shrugging. "Over time, I started thinking…well, Krid got into my head before, and told me what ship to get on, leaving my daughter behind, my surgeon job, everything. He could do that again."

Merne reminded her, "We told you Krid's being monitored. Besides, if he put that idea in your mind, of her on that moon, then you wouldn't be leading him to her by going there. You'd just be going where he sent you."

Tlalit added to her partner's point. "Krid can't control minds without being detected."

"You're sure about that?" Yanda mumbled, too low for Tlalit to hear. To Merne, she responded, "You asked what Seiti said. I wasn't able to get much from her. I asked who's taking care of her, where she's staying. When she finally spoke, she begged me to take her with me. I had to tell her I was there in spirit only, would have to find where she really is." Yanda's throat tightened. "But someone could have created all that in my mind." She heaved a shuddering breath and stared at her screen, haunted by her daughter's voice, so real, so familiar.

"And you've had no contact since?" Merne asked. The elf woman, hundreds of years old but appearing young middle-aged, had braided her brown-green hair in tendrils that crowned her head and dangled in sprays around her face. Her skin was a velvet green and gold, her eyes brown with gold flecks like the big cats Yanda had seen in vids and pics.

"I made contact during the great mind-meld of Withum ceremony. You know how powerful that is."

Their minds all traveled to memories of the yearly festival when forest and sea elves gather on the shore of Terlond and linked minds in a great connection brought on by the blossoming of the withum flower.

"I haven't tried to do it alone." Yanda scooted to lean her back against the couch. "I wouldn't know where to start. Could you help me?"

"Hmm…" Merne contemplated.

Yanda's chest ached from weeks of terror for her little girl. Ever since Tlalit and Merne had caught a feed on the universal web of a girl Seiti's age on a moon frequented by traffickers, she'd been mad with fear for her. She'd dropped into the dark sea of the Neyla elves to get help from their great Stone, Ash-Don. Then had this vision. It seemed like the only clue to follow so she, allied with sea and woodland elves, and her Mingal waterworld friend, Vatu, had set out.

Why'd you run off, my sweet Seiti?

Mnenu's eyes darted from them to the plaz toys he fit together with Zami. He turned to Merne. "Ash-don thinks the moon might be familiar."

"But what's the chance it's their sister moon? Unless they felt it." Yanda held slight hope. "They'd have a lot of incentive to help us, if it meant making contact with their sibling stone."

They'd only been out a few days, which had mostly been spent learning how to live on the ship together for a long voyage, and planning food stops. Before leaving, they'd created a lap pool for Mnenu, filled with Terlondian waters, refreshed by living mollusks at the bottom and sides. Being Mnenu's area of study, he'd relished the project. Wanting to understand the workings of the ship, Tlalit made him second-in-command on board.

The group had gone round and round about the route they should take. Some directions had solar storms, or flying rock debris.

"We should take Vatu home first," Yanda insisted.

"I want to help you. We can all go to Mingal after," Vatu kept saying.

"It's a risk, going into Unknown Space, if there are

even any ships that can," Yanda responded. "There are no outposts. No supply stations—"

"—that we know of," Mnenu indicated.

"You said you got coordinates when we located Tenali?" Yanda asked Merne.

"I don't know why he thinks he's in direct line with where Seiti is," Merne answered.

Tlalit chimed in, "I got coordinates. As the Withum was wearing off, I put in points I recognized and triangulated." She came to the doorway and leaned on the jamb, grinning with the memory. "You know how we were seeing everything at once? Understanding the whole universe?"

The others responded, revery in their voices; with the two Stones involved, it had been the most intense Withum ceremony in recent memory.

"But Tenali's not there now," Tlalit declared. "He moved. I've been pinging him and he seems unreachable."

"You don't think he went into Unknown Space...?" Merne was grim.

"Communication doesn't penetrate there," Tlalit said, turning back to check the controls.

"Exactly. He wouldn't risk..." Merne's voice trailed away.

Three weeks into their journey, it was Mnenu's turn to monitor the controls. Yanda kept him company, attention partly on the panels as she played a game with Zami having to do with the stars.

An encrypted message alert popped up in the corner of her ENAC screen. She sat bolt upright. Tapping on it, she saw it was from Ilan, the big, red-haired, enigmatic Qontaqian man who'd been her staunch and only reliable ally on that treacherous trip to the Allandian outback, trying to find leads regarding her daughter's location among rebels hiding there.

No message opened.

"I need to ask Tlalit how to open this message from Ilan," Yanda said, standing. Tlalit and Merne were taking a break in the deep, narrow, salt-water pool that resembled sea caves, with live plants growing at the edges.

"Why don't you ask me?" Mnenu's face soured, wounded.

"Oh. Do you know about... I didn't know you—"

Mnenu laughed. "Just kidding. I have some skill on computer but nothing like Tlalit and Merne."

Yanda smacked his shoulder.

He grabbed her hand and kissed the palm, sending tingles. "You go ahead and ask them."

"I'll send Vatu to keep you company."

"Not necessary. I'm a big boy." His hang-dog face said something different.

"That you are." She stepped into the lounge area where Vatu was on her lalut—the elegant, compact device of the Mingal. "I'm going up to ask Tlalit something."

Vatu set down her *lalut* and crawled toward Zami. "Let's play hide the turtle."

Yanda gave her a grateful glance and headed for the elevator.

On the spa level, Yanda opened the door to a romantic grotto replete with twinkly lights and scented oils. Tlalit and Merne looked like jewels entwined in the water, deep in...conversation.

Embarrassed to interrupt, she stood poolside, shifting from one foot to the other, breathing in the fecund smells of lush plants and aromatic candles. Water lapping and low conversation were the only sounds, except for the ever-present hum of the ship. But it really was urgent. She cleared her throat. "Ah-hem. Sorry to disturb your…nice time."

Tlalit's tangerine cockatiel-peaked hair disappeared under the water and bobbed up next to her. "No problem, little sister."

Yanda sat at the edge. "It's Ilan. I think he's sending an urgent message but it doesn't open. I'm pretty sure it's encrypted." She tilted the ENAC so Tlalit could see the screen. Merne joined them and looked as well.

Tlalit tilted her head to one side in thought. "Chances are, Ilan will make you fetch a code only you can find." She used her teacher voice. "What program have you been using for AI?"

The ship always gave a gentle vibration and hummed. Yanda shut out awareness of all else. Tapping the Da-Lam icon, Yanda closed her eyes and let her connection travel in. When she opened, grids were expanding into the air, holographically. Ilan appeared.

She felt a surge of warmth, seeing his big, strong, worried face.

"You're not far from Qontaq," he said, voice tired but the low, rich timbre was deeply familiar. "I need you to get Bonden. Well, me and Bonden."

Yanda glanced at Tlalit who said, "He's right. We're not far."

"Can we go there?" Yanda asked the captain.

"Of course. Sounds dire," Tlalit responded. "Bonden's a sister from your captivity. You have to save her."

Yanda asked Ilan, "What's going on there? Can you talk?"

"I can."

"Is it safe to approach Qontaq? Well, you'll work that out with Tlalit." Yanda turned the screen away so it faced the two female elves in the pool. Discussion ensued, much of which consisted of numbers. Yanda set the ENAC in her lap, ready for a long stay.

"Let's get out," Tlalit said.

Mnenu texted, "Are we taking a turn in the honeymoon grotto?"

"Maybe. Have you been listening?" Yanda tsk-tsk'ed by text.

"A little. We have to divert. Ilan and Bonden are in trouble."

"You *did* listen."

"A little," he thought to her, sheepish.

Tlalit broke into their shared mind space, walking toward her towel. "I'll free Mnenu to come up here. Water's nice. Renewing."

Mnenu posted an icon to Yanda of a leering bubble face.

"Shall I dry you?" Yanda asked Tlalit, who stood nearby, looking down from her near seven-foot height.

"Yes, please." Tlalit tossed the towel onto a chair.

Using the trick she'd learned from the Neyla sea elves—a skill only obtained once they mastered *lanten* transformation into sea creature—Yanda wrapped her hand around the elf's leg and Tlalit dried instantly, even her hair which she reshaped into the familiar a cockatiel peak.

"That's *cratat*," the techie whiz said, grinning as she

donned the captain suit she loved wearing. It was made of a flexible silvery plaz and had the *Sarsefi* insignia, stars forming a tree.

Merne got the same drying treatment from Yanda, then slipped into a yellow lounging outfit that form-fitted her tall figure with soft give. He appeared in the doorway holding three-year-old Zami. Merne and Tlalit squeezed past them as they left, giving kisses to Merne's grandson. Vatu was not far behind.

Yanda, Mnenu, Vatu and Zami soaked in a hot tub that curved at the end of the long lap pool. Vatu dove from it for a lap, then invited Zami to swim one with her. She and the toddler gave kisses before Vatu took him to their sleeping cells on the lower floor, promising to snuggle him to sleep, leaving Yanda and Mnenu alone. Zami loved her as a second mother and put up no objection.

Yanda dove into the deep end. Mnenu came up from below her and they swam together, long languid strokes. Yanda turned toward him and found a warm kiss awaiting her.

"Are you glad you came along on this journey?" she asked.

"So far," he said, expression giving nothing away.

CHAPTER

2

Yanda turned over and snaked an arm around Mnenu who slept faced away. Ambient light increased, replicating the morning hour and she gazed at what the Sea Elf had chosen to bring: numerous plants and shells that rushed with the sound of waves, a sea horse tapestry on the wall. Yanda noticed a slightly salty scent emanating from the fabric, reminding her of the Terlondian seas.

Quietly she slid from bed, dressed and left, while Mnenu slept through the first bells signaling the earliest crew shifts.

On the main level, she found Merne, Vatu, and Zami in the kitchen enjoying hot cups of kran—*chaka* in Zami's case—with muffins.

"Did you sleep well?" Merne asked.

Yanda poured *kaffe*. Mouth full of muffin she mumbled, "Um. Not a whole lot."

Vatu smirked. Yanda sat and elbowed her. All innocence, she asked Merne, "How was your night?"

"De-licious. A late swim is the best for deep slumber."

Pouring creamy high-chlorophyl plant milk into her *kaffe*, she sipped. They'd developed special plant milks for Zami after their first space flight from Terlond to Alland, when Soni had run diagnostics on both of them and found that any extended time away from plants could injure Zami's metabolism. Being half forest-elf, he needed high chlorophyl foods and lights, and as much exposure to plants as possible. They'd been growing foliage throughout the ship, on wall scaffolding with special lights and auto-watering. Tlalit kept adding drip systems.

Getting up, Merne put her dishes in auto-clean and, bidding them a good morning, left to join Tlalit in the command center.

After a few bites, Yanda said, "I'll check the ship since Mnenu seems to be catching up on z's."

"Wore him out, did you?" Vatu grinned impishly.

Yanda gave her a shocked laugh. "Whatever could you mean?" She wrapped the rest of her muffin in a beeswax cloth and crammed it into a utility pocket in her coverall.

Vatu pushed back and swung Zami into her arms. "I'll take this guy to wash and get a bit of schooling in the lounge."

Yanda kissed her cheek, then Zami's. "Thanks. I'll be back in no time." She left the kitchen, and in the hall, entered hidden stairs and galley ways that traversed the workings of the space vessel. Leaving the main level that housed the control room, lounge, greenhouse and kitchen, she skirted the sleeping quarters one floor up, checking for warning lights, and, on to the area next to the spa room with its lap pool, the top level. Finding no problems, she descended narrow stairways, back the way she'd come, past the central level to below decks, where storage and engine spaces were located.

"That doesn't look good." Noticing a sickly yellow light on one of the air-duct sensors, she climbed into the chute, one-person wide, leading to an outer hatch through several sections divided by sphincter material, securing oxygen to lesser and lesser degrees. In one of the outer sections, she heard a rip and cool air touched her skin. Yanda's suit was snagged. On what? Metal protruding? She arched her head to try to see but the quarters were too tight. She tried to scoot backward but was hung up. She slowed her breathing and sent a mental call to Mnenu, "You up?"

He replied immediately. "What's wrong?"

"I'm stuck."

"Be there *sondo*." In no time, it meant in the Neyla sea-elf language.

She could tell he'd jumped into the pool for a quick swim to wake himself up. It seemed harder and harder for him to maintain his energy. She saw in his mind as he leapt from the pool, his one-piece suit drying as he ran.

Moments later, he crawled in behind her and ran searching fingers up her sides.

She snorted a laugh. "That tickles."

Not finding the hitch, he wiggled up until their bodies were partly entwined.

"That's the idea," he mouthed into her stomach, his chin wagging more than necessary, making her squirm.

"Stop. You'll make me pee."

"That's okay," he said, shaking with laughter. "I think

I found it. Ooh, that's not good. A rough edge popping out." He fumbled her fabric loose from the catch.

"Too bad I didn't see that."

"You'll have some mending to do. Actually, it's good you discovered it. I'll come back with tools." He started wedging his way back out. "Don't kick me!"

They were wracked with laughter by the time they wormed their way back to the small engine room, light-headed from low oxygen. They'd already been in there too long. Yanda's hair stood out a foot with electricity, driving Mnenu to new gales of jollity.

"I got a reading for clogged air-duct," Yanda explained after deep breaths in healthy oxygen levels. "I didn't even get to the problematic conduit."

"Did you have a vacuum with you?" he asked.

With an insulted humph, she slid the long thin tool from a pocket, next to the one with her smashed muffin.

"It might be one of the bigger ducts. I'll bring more tools with me. Go fix your suit." He grinned, flipping the fabric near her butt as he turned her, kissed the top of her head and gave her a soft push. "Looks good, though. New style."

"Very funny." She reached back to hold the gape shut, glancing at his strangely handsome face with its dark and light green hues. "Thanks for saving me."

"Oh, you could have gotten out. You'd just have made a much bigger rip."

"I could have unhooked myself if it wasn't too tight for my arms."

"We should get Vatu to do these. She'd fit easily." He rummaged for tools hanging above a work bench.

"I'm sure she'd be happy to. She's better with low-oxygen, too. Doesn't mind at all."

"Hmm. I could go lanten. But I don't think as clearly for this type of thing. I guess I could train myself."

He was still mumbling when she exited, climbed plaz steps to more hospitable atmosphere on the upper floors. In her room, she put on her second favorite outfit and grabbed a sewing kit.

In the lounge, Zami squealed to see her. Yanda dropped the torn fabric and kit on a couch and rolled with him on the rug.

"What happened? Did you split a seam?" Vatu wondered.

"No. I tried to fix an air duct and caught on something. Mnenu's going to go back and see what I snagged on, and fix the duct."

Vatu set her device down. "Should we be worried?"

"I don't think it's serious but Mnenu will give us a report. How about Swoopers?" Yanda said to Zami, pulling out a green box.

"Swim?" he asked.

"Let's save the pool for evening, okay?"

"Yes." Zami looked eager, peering at the game which they hadn't played.

"I'm going to get lots of water time on this trip, with all the pool enthusiasts." Yanda grinned at Vatu.

"I'll see if Tlalit needs anything. She's such a stoic." Vatu stood.

"You're so thoughtful. What about you? What do you need?" Yanda called to her.

Vatu waved a "don't be silly" hand on her way across to the control room next door.

With his eyes focused, Zami made the box lid float off, then cards swoop up and land in his hands.

"You're going to get lazy doing everything with your mind," she said, assembling a plaz structure, then taking the deck of cards from him and sliding them into a chute.

"I'll have a strong mind though, right?" he said.

She gazed at him, her finger poised over a button on the Swooper side which gleamed in several colors. "Are you really only three?"

"Four pretty soon, if we're following the Terlondian calendar."

"Even sooner with the Alland one." Though I'm not sure that's your native planet, she thought. She refused to accept Terlond as his home world. That gave his father, the Elf Zamani, more right to keep him in the elven forest.

A voice that hadn't been there for many months came into her head. Bonden. Calling out for help. Immediately the Hive Minds gathered — the ten fems who'd been in captivity together for a year and a half. They'd been free for nearly as long, as Yanda searched for her daughter.

Bonden's anguish pained Yanda so she nearly doubled over, but she pressed her palms to the carpet, forcing a smile for Zami. Yanda put a hand on her son's arm so she could stay connected with him while her mind was elsewhere — as much to comfort her as to protect him.

Having spent his first months with these female humanoids with powers from throughout the universe, he'd be easily susceptible to receiving the mind-meld but she tried to shield him. In Bonden's mind, Yanda could see where she was: a cell with barbarous chains, dark patches she tried to imagine were not blood.

She pictured the earnest, husky engineer who'd brought them through thirty-feet of solid rock to escape Krid, captured in that filth. She hitched a sob. "I thought you were out," Yanda said across lightyears, throat tight. "Ilan asked us to come and get both of you. He didn't say you were—" How could they get her loose? Yanda wondered. Who held her, and what would they encounter to set her free? Briefly, she also thought, "I have to get my daughter. I can't be doing this."

Through clenched teeth, Bonden said, "He thought he'd have me out, I'm sure. Cocky bastard."

She tried to laugh but coughed instead, a wet cough. Yanda sensed through Bonden's mind the collar around her neck that dampened her powers.

"Are you on Tlalit's ship?" Bonden asked.

Yanda affirmed.

"I doubt if even they can find the schematics to this place." Bonden's voice was faint. Weak and in pain, she slumped against a scarred, stained surface behind her. "You have to look through the walls, Yanda. I hate to ask it. That's probably why Ilan called to you and not fellow Qontaqians."

"Through multiple walls?" Yanda balked. Her sight was strong but she hadn't been able to see into the rock labyrinth to find an escape. She could see down or over one layer at a time.

"If Shouma could amplify," Bonden said, "I think she could boost whatever you do." There was slight hope, but more desperation, in Bonden's tone.

"I'm here," Shouma said.

"Where are you physically?" Yanda asked. "Not on Qontaq, are you?"

"I'm in the same star system, with my son's family. My nephew's a trader here and has ships with a lot of capabilities."

"Like what?" Yanda said. "What does he trade?" She put a grin into her question.

Ilan joined their minds. "I can support both of you without you entering into Qontaq's atmosphere. You don't want to land here. There's a lot of unrest. You should stay behind the closest moon." This last he directed to Tlalit. The mind-meld had grown to include many of their group, some in far distant locations.

"I've got the closest moon's coordinates," Tlalit said. "We'll head that way."

Yanda sensed Bonden's tears welling reading the emotion in her mind as she took in the news that they were coming.

Like a quick embrace, the hive-mind squeezed briefly, then released, a promise to be on-call understood.

Yanda checked in with Zami. "How are you, cookie? Done eating? Want to get out?"

Zami nodded and tried to slide down beneath the tray rigged to the table. She hoisted him up and carried him into the lounge, where he had cabinets filled with toys. As he rummaged for his favorites, she flopped into a giant pillow-chair and reconnected with Shouma by mind. "Where are you? Who else is with you?"

Shouma sipped tea. "A lot of us are here on Sandu, my son's planet."

She had only recently shared with her that none of her children had ever been to Erzon, the famous planet of the powerful Sonda people—Shouma's clan.

"Chela came to help heal my niece," Shouma explained. "The Jejods have been here waiting for transport. Beri—"

"Beri's there?" Yanda did not expect this. The last they spoke, he'd wanted to get back to his home planet,

Romden. He'd not seen his family since before their captivity together on Farn.

"He met someone." Shouma smirked fondly.

"Oh." Yanda wondered about that. Male? Female? They were friends but she'd sometimes thought he might have wanted more from her. He never said or did anything to make her think that but there was something in his eyes at times. "And Chin? Is she there, too?"

"Chin says she doesn't go home." Shouma let that hang without explanation.

Where was Chin's home, anyway? The big warrior-trained fem had never said, and Yanda hadn't asked. So much time together and so much she had never sought to know.

"For the time being, she's staying wherever the Jejods are."

"Dele must be back on Qontaq," Yanda guessed.

"No. She, too, met someone. Ran off to Prokit's Moon, I think. Tell me about you, Yanda. Your daughter?"

Yanda's throat tightened. "She's what our journey is about. Seiti left Alland looking for me. I went to Ash-Don for help finding her and, at Withum, we had a collective vision of Seiti on a moon in Unknown Space. But I don't know if it's real. I mean, how could it be?"

Shouma tsked sympathy. "You're not going into Unknown Space, are you?"

Vatu had come in and settled on her favorite couch. "Can I join?" She tapped her temple.

Yanda nodded. "Tenali's ship was at the edge of the Known when we had the vision. He thought he was aligned with, or close to, the moon where my daughter might be."

"Not that far from Mingal," Vatu added.

Yanda smiled at her, then shrugged. "It was very dreamlike. I don't know if my daughter's there at all." The more solid the trip became, the less she trusted the likelihood. The fact that the Stones saw it with them and believed in its truth was her main touchstone now.

"You have to believe in these messages," Shouma told Yanda. "You have nothing else to go on, do you? So, you'll head to where Tenali was? That means you'll go home now, Vatu?"

"Maybe." Vatu played with her head nubs, a habit when certain uncomfortable questions arose.

"Child, what are you running from?" Shouma asked. "Oh, here's Tedro. Let me find out about the possibility of immediate departure to Belsom."

Yanda wasn't surprised Shouma had plucked the name of the moon from Tlalit. "Okay. Talk soon." Yanda hated to let Shouma go. It had been comforting to feel the woman's powerful motherly presence.

Vatu made a pouty face, clearly sharing the emotion. Pulling out of mind-meld, they gazed at each other for a moment, hands clenched in their laps. They'd grown used to worrying together this way.

Vatu chewed a nail. "That's distressing. About Bonden."

Yanda nodded. "At least Tlalit is willing to go there."

"Do you think we can save her?" Vatu asked.

Yanda thought a moment. "Ilan seems like he can do anything."

"But he didn't succeed."

"He needs us." There was little Shouma and the other fems couldn't do, Yanda thought.

Merne came in from the control room and sat on the remaining couch that curved in an S.

Stretching on her side, she pulled a transparent screen in front of her, fingers sweeping so that locations showed on maps in the air, dots and numbers appearing in varying colors on them.

"How long?" Yanda asked.

"Hold on," Merne said as she made calculations.

Mnenu returned from rounds inspecting the ship. "Want to fill me in?" He folded himself on the rug near where Zami played, leaning against Yanda's pillow chair.

"Bonden's captive in a place of torment." To ease her worry, Yanda pulled a handful of Mnenu's hair between her shaking fingers and proceeded to braid it, the motion and downy texture calming her.

He reached back and stroked her arm. "That's awful. Qontaqis have her?"

"I assume. Ilan doesn't think we should land on Qontaq so we'll try to get help from Belsom, the closest moon. I guess they need me to see through multiple walls, though I'm not sure I can. From behind a moon? I have a feeling I'll have to find a way onto the planet."

"Which is dangerous," Vatu said, holding Yanda's eyes in a steady gaze.

Yanda shrugged. "Well, I'm still going. It's Bonden."

"Where's Ilan?" Mnenu asked.

"I don't know. Hiding on Qontaq, I assume. Bonden said he probably thought he could get her out. He can take on any identity, even the mind-register. Like Vatu."

A faint tinge of turquoise moved through Vatu's head-nubs, indicating pleasure or pride.

"I doubt if I can do all Ilan does," Vatu said, modestly.

"I do it to keep unseen where I think he can probably be very powerful, imposing, with his ability. I'm just guessing because of the…potent energy that comes from him."

"He's impressive," Mnenu turned to look at Yanda, his hair now in a neat cornrow on each side. "He tried and it didn't work? What happened?"

"I haven't talked to him since he spoke with Tlalit last night. He only said, 'Come get us.' I'll see what I can find out." Yanda shoved out of the voluminous chair, wanting to talk with Ilan alone. She was fond of the big redhead Qontaqian. He could be overbearing, but cared so fiercely. That was hard to resist in an often-hostile universe where no place felt like home. And now he and Bonden were in peril.

Mnenu's eyes followed her as she started across the room. She turned. "Zami, show Mnenu what you're making. I'll be right back."

"Let me see, buddy," he said, though his dark intense eyes questioned her, detecting her desire to be alone to contact the Qontaqian man.

CHAPTER

3

The door shooshed closed behind her and she climbed the narrow stairs to their berths level. Entering the narrow hall, she stopped at the third door on the left, an equivalent row on the right. Once inside, she coded the door in locked position, wanting a moment completely to herself—why, she couldn't have said.

Dropping the lower bunk, she tossed herself on it, rolled on her side and sent her mind to Ilan, pressing through heavy shielding. His mental register was keyed into her psyche, allowing her where few would find an opening. She tapped. "Are you safe?"

"Not entirely," came his tired reply.

"You didn't tell us Bonden is still a prisoner."

In his mind, Yanda saw his hand come up, push back glasses and rub his swollen, gritty eyes.

Not getting an answer, Yanda expressed Bonden's suspicion. "You tried to get her out and couldn't."

"I need your help." The thought was sluggish, as if he reserved energy.

"I'm surprised I have a skill you Qontaqians lack," Yanda said, honestly perplexed.

"You'd be surprised what you have, Yanda."

"I know. Xentu blood." She all but groaned.

"Well...?"

She fought her usual frustration with the Xentu card. Since no one had ever taught her about her Xentu heritage, she could do little with the expectations that seemed to come with it. "What's the plan," she asked, "once we hide behind the moon? And if I can't help from there, what next?"

"Let's come to that when we get there. I have ideas."

"We've got Shouma, Vatu, Merne—they can all disguise or be invisible, even make others unseen."

"I don't want to endanger any of them."

"Neither do I, but Shouma can amplify our energy better close up. She's on her way."

"I have a plan. The more of you behind that moon, the better."

"What did you try already?"

"If this works, we'll have lots of time for me to recount my previous efforts."

She detected his self-effacing disgust. "Efforts? As in, more than one? How long have you been at this?" More uneasy, Yanda sat up and leaned against the wall.

"'Night, honey. I'm beat."

"Okay, we'll talk soon. Hopefully very soon."

"Righto." Ilan's mind slipped from hers, leaving an impenetrable blank.

Yanda traced stitches on a wall hanging she'd obtained from artisans in the outback of Alland depicting village life.

These were the rustic home towns of people she'd met at Pedore, where culture had remained rich, and in ways untouched. A marsupial-like Nic-Nic clung to a branch in the foreground. She'd thought of Zami when she purchased it. At least Merne had brought her tiny primate, Tuk-Tuk, along on the ship. Animals were Zami's passion. And this one was special, with sentient powers Zami read better than anyone.

The situation with Bonden was terrifying, rivaling her fears for her daughter in its assault on her nerves. She remained alone on her bed a moment longer, then descended to join the others. "Anyone hungry?" she called into the lounge from the kitchen.

Merne moseyed in. "I can sauté the few remaining hydroponic mushrooms and make animal-shaped patties for Zami."

"He'd love that." Yanda said, pulling out flour and veggies from the refrigeration unit.

Rummaging in a dry bin, Merne mumbled, "Hopefully we can stock up on Belsom."

Others drifted in and helped fix the meal, each contributing to making ship food as palatable as possible by combining fresh items they'd grown onboard with carefully parceled out supplies obtained at space stations. Vatu made her signature seaweed balls; Mnenu dug into his precious stock of ocean *lilin* syrup for gravy.

"But is there no part of Qontaq we can go to for supplies? Maybe far from this prison cell?" Vatu complained as she scraped the last of her golly powder for thickening.

Tlalit's voice came over the intercom from the flight deck. "Though small, Belsom is a market moon. There will be some supplies."

Conversation fell into what was needed on the ship,

including engine parts. Later in the day, Shouma called to all who'd been in the mind-meld the day before. "My son found space on a clipper taking medical supplies to Qontaq."

"Sandu is in the same star system as Qontaq, right?" Vatu asked.

"It is," Shouma confirmed.

"But Sandu's not your home planet." Yanda was confused.

"Remember she went to Sandu to help her granddaughter?" Vatu reminded Yanda. "Is Chela with you?" she asked Shouma.

"I'd like to leave Chela with my granddaughter if she's not needed for this mission. Hopefully Bonden won't need more than my skills." Shouma seemed tired, her communication sagging.

Yanda was disappointed. Bonden would need healing. Shouma, too, was a fine herbalist but her greatest talents lay in mind-work and she usually needed her energy for that. "Well, we don't know how badly Bonden is hurt but she seemed…" Yanda searched for a gentle enough word not to alarm but to convey the need, "…ailing,"

"Let's bring her back to Sandu on a medical transport. There are advanced hospitals and research facilities here," Shouma suggested. "I could bring her and you could go on with your journey."

Yanda had allowed herself to hope Shouma might spend some time with them. Chela as well. They'd been like aunties from Zami's birth and for all the time they'd been in captivity together. He'd missed them and often asked about them. But she shouldn't be greedy. "It'll be good to see you," she said to Shouma. "I'll let Ilan know so we can plan for meeting up."

"Let's all stay together," Tlalit proposed.

"I'm here," Ilan's presence was weak, even dim.

"Are you okay? You're faint."

"I'm doing all I can to shield myself. You're aiming to meet Shouma on Belsom sometime tomorrow."

"Is that right, Tlalit?" Yanda asked their captain.

"Short nano-jumps can be hard on the body," Ilan said to Shouma.

"They have a wonderful stasis system," Shouma extolled. "Very robust. I think I'll be fine. Do we have anything new on Bonden? Are you with us, Bonden?"

They stayed quiet, trying to find her voice in their minds.

"I don't hear her. Do you, Ilan?" Yanda asked.

There was a pause. Yanda thought they'd lost Ilan as well, but at last he said, barely discernable, "I don't." His barely detectible mental voice seemed weary and discouraged.

"Try to keep confidence, friend," Yanda said, her throat tightening. "We're doing all we can."

"I'd better go," Ilan said, and was gone.

Shouma said, "I've asked about Dipuk. She's doing well. Chela can be spared for a short time. Hopefully we'll have Bonden out quickly."

Yanda was not all that confident but hid her attitude. Briefly, she wondered why Chela had not yet gone home.

"If your granddaughter takes a dip, we can send Chela back," Tlalit said, sounding affirmative as always.

Yanda wished she had developed such unflagging assurance of her own abilities. Mnenu wrapped an arm around her as if sensing melancholy.

Yanda said to the group, "Okay, I guess we should maintain our usual routines until we are approaching

Belsom and then can make contact."

Minds parted. Yanda turned to study Mnenu's face. "Have you gotten in any swimming today?" The deeper streaks in the dark and light greens of his complexion worried her. Was the extended time on shipboard harming him?

"Yes, I have. Why do you ask?" He bent to nuzzle her neck. "Am I less pleasing to you this way?"

She snugged her bent leg onto his lap, and leaned in for a kiss. "Are you kidding?" She meant it. He was always appealing, maybe more mysterious this way. "I just worry about the long journey."

"That's why Tlalit installed the special pool."

"Are we keeping enough chlorophyll in the air? I wish we had Soni and her Flari here. She's expert at healing, adjusting the waters."

"Where is Soni?" Mnenu asked. He ran a finger up her arm, sending sweet shivers.

"In Pedore, that refuge in my hometown. We should maybe send you back with Bonden to Sandu to make sure you're okay. You could go home if—"

"Shh." He put a finger on her lips, making intense tingles bloom deep in her belly.

"Keep this up and we'll have to…retire to a bed chamber," she whispered.

"A swim would be therapeutic, I think." His eyes glowed with desire.

"Oh, all right," Yanda conceded as if reluctant, her nether regions saying something different.

Vatu, curled in a huge round pillow-chair reading to Zami.

"We're going to take a dip," Yanda told her. "Want to come?"

"We're good. I think Zami's fading toward a nap." Vatu pulled the child closer, his head on her shoulder, relaxed and content.

As they climbed the stairs, Mnenu asked, "What will you do when Vatu returns to Mingal?"

"She didn't seem to want to leave your fine sea city," Yanda pointed out as she opened to the tropical air of the pool room.

"True," Mnenu responded, stripping off his one-piece ship suit. "But she and Zami are very close. As are you two."

"I know." Naked, she dove into the pool. When she popped her head up, she said, "I guess we'll cross that bridge..."

Mnenu came up next to her. "Guess we will." His eyes conveyed that was not the topic he wanted to pursue.

The greenhouse room glowed with sun-like light that moved through the day as though the lights had their own orbit. The walls were lattices covered in vines. Insects that ate troublesome bugs made faint clicking sounds. Water dripped among the plants where spray moistened the leaves.

Yanda sat at a worktable in the middle, tucking in starts for various greens and foods that would sustain them during the long journey. They were even growing berries, round and orange, and pumpkin-like legumes pumpkins that sprawled across raised beds. Below these, shade plants such as the brassicas, parsley, rhubarb, and mushrooms, thrived in moist darkness.

Vatu squatted at the compost tea barrel, switching on the arms to move it around before gathering some to spray. "I like it in here," Vatu said when there had been a stretch of silence.

"Me, too." Yanda grinned. "It's peaceful."

"And rewarding. It feels like everything we do in here will feed us or do us some good."

"Just being in here does us good," Yanda said. "What is food growing like on Mingal?"

"Oh. Well. We still eat a lot straight from the sea and the caves. We have cave greenhouses something like this room. We also have cave orchards. Delicacies have been adopted from other places, like night fruits from Ontil, Takmik's planet. We imported them, started our own orchards. They're beautiful."

"What makes them pretty?" Yanda asked.

"There's a moth that actually helps the trees and it glows at night. The walls of the cave have phosphorescence in places. So the orchard has subtle light playing through it. Especially good if you have night sight." She turned off the tap and squirted some areas with a spray bottle.

"I'd like to see that."

When they came out with harvest in bowls, they found Merne in the kitchen giving Zami a math lesson using slices of fruits and nuts.

"He's too smart for this," Merne said with a proud grin. "We'll have him helping Tlalit soon."

"He does help me," Tlalit said over the com unit. She had every part of the ship connected and would probably keep them all open if she had a choice.

"You know what we've said about eavesdropping." Merne pretended to be irritated.

Tlalit ignored that. "He solved a quadratic I was puzzling over the other day."

"Did you ask him for help or did he just happen to be in your head?" Merne asked, moving *santu fruit* pieces into a new configuration for the child.

"Oh, I ask him questions sometimes to see what he'll say," Tlalit answered.

"I'll bring fruit to you," Yanda told Tlalit. She filled a bowl with bright berries before leaving the kitchen.

In the control room, Yanda set the bowl on a pull-out tray near Tlalit. Then she sat in a swivel chair and gazed out at passing nebulae, admiring the colors teal and fuchsia. She hadn't seen outer space until she was in her thirties, well into her surgery profession.

She turned to Tlalit. "So, other than quadratic equations, what types of questions do you ask Zami?" She felt, as his mother, she had a right to know. And she was curious.

Tlalit studied her a moment. "Mostly philosophical. Or semi-scientific, though I guess it might be considered spiritual, too. 'Why do mushrooms like the dark?' 'If you were a *woo-loo*, where would you live?' That sort of thing."

"So just when you're bored in here watching the stars and your panels?" Yanda asked, bringing a leg up into the chair and settling more comfortably.

"Generally. But sometimes a question comes to me."

"Do you ask anyone else questions like that, or just Zami?"

"Mostly Zami."

"He gives you rewarding answers?" Yanda asked.

"Always."

"Why do you think that is?"

They had forgotten that the coms were on and open. Those in the kitchen listened, glancing at each other.

"He has a good mind. And a good mind at age three has special ways of looking at things. This isn't unusual, Yandawi. We do this a lot in Elf culture. It stimulates the children, brings them into the fold of our community, and adds their voices to the ways we're thinking."

That reassured Yanda. "That's always been the way?"

"As far as I know. That might be a Zamani question."

"Or Decru," Yanda suggested since he was oldest Elf she knew of.

"Yes! I'd forgotten that you met him when we fought Krid."

"He left an impression on me. Big energy."

"He would." Tlalit had a half smile, as though reminiscing.

Merne came to the doorway carrying a *ralashal* game set in a carved box. "Can I join you? Am I interrupting?"

Mnenu, Vatu, and Zami entered after her and pulled out a drop-down table for the game.

"Interesting conversation about children," Mnenu said.

"You left the com on." Yanda didn't really mind. She popped a berry in her mouth and helped set up the game thinking that would help take her mind off worries.

CHAPTER

4

Yanda woke to find a message on her ENAC from Shouma. Putting on a robe, she gathered a still sleeping Zami in her arms and followed the lines of lights in dark halls to the kitchen module.

Since keeping comfortable gravity taxed the ship resources, the living area was small: a number of narrow sleeping cabins, kitchen, lounge, compact bathrooms and the control room.

Dragging a comfy chair from the lounge into the kitchen, Yanda settled Zami in with pillow and blanket. The child slumbered on as she made herself *kaffe*.

The crew produced plant milks thickened with chia powder and oil. She hunched at the table over her ENAC, sipping from her steaming cup.

Shouma's transport turned out to be as swift as promised. She'd already landed on Belsom and lodged at an inn near a cozy café, she wrote. "I'll be here when you get here.

Shamba's Nook." Or the inn The Wayfarer. There's only the one main city here, Lantat."

Yanda wrote back. "Have you contacted Ilan?"

"Tried to."

"No luck?" Yanda's heart squeezed with worry. She sent a quick mind-message to Tlalit. "Shouma's on Belsom. How far are we?"

Tlalit responded, "I'm thinking we'll do hyperdrive soon, though the engine needs refilling of some vital fluids. It's down, but I figure we have enough."

"Estimate if we do use hyperdrive?"

"A few hours, I'm hoping."

"Okay. Shouma hasn't been able to reach Ilan. I'm—"

"Worried. Yeah," Tlalit responded.

The rest got the message to ready for stasis pods.

"What about you?" Yanda asked Tlalit.

"I'll set the coordinates and begin hyperdrive, then climb into mine."

"Then no one will be watching for hazards or—"

"The ship has protections for warp speed and the possibility of collision. I paid extra for the latest air cushions, sensors, and warning devices, which will wake me if need be, at the same time turning off hyperdrive." She grinned. "All good questions. It makes sense to worry, and I should have explained."

"Thank you." Despite the information, Yanda felt a sort of grim fatalism about the situation. In the narrow hallway of sleeping modules, she said to Merne, "Can I have Zami in my stasis pod with me?"

"He'll be fine. We can put you right next to him and set it so you get the alarm and are released from stasis if any readings are off on his."

"There're enough for one each," Mnenu said. "What about if we take on passengers, though?"

"Ilan and Bonden, for instance." Tlalit understood his meaning. "In the upper area, near the pool and greenhouse are several more."

"Good thing these are built tall for Elves." Yanda was trying to be casual and conversational but her heart sent an aching pulse into her throat. "There could even be Chin and the Jejods. Will we have enough?"

"Some are collapsed in the reserve room," Tlalit said. "They set up pretty quickly."

Zami put his palm to Yanda's cheek. "It's okay, Mama. Auntie Tlalit's ship will take care of us."

She touched his cheek. "You'll have to take care of your worry-wort momma," she said, sitting him on the edge of the closest stasis bed. "I'll be in the one under you."

Mnenu hopped up to the third bed, above them. "And I'll be above! You'll be in a sandwich, kiddo."

Zami giggled. "Okay." He flopped into the bed.

Yanda started settling him, straightening out padding. "Before you know it, you'll be waking up on Belsom. We'll see a new place!" Her heart stuck in her throat, worrying about this trip and Ilan's silence, not to mention Bonden.

"Here, let me help." Merne adjusted straps.

Tlalit squeezed in and tickled Zami on his sides. He gave a throaty chuckle. The tangerine-haired elf looked over the dials, expression turning serious.

"Okay, now you." Tlalit swept her arm toward the lower stasis bunk.

Yanda kissed Zami and climbed in below. She'd traveled in stasis before, in a drug-induced fog, when she'd been abducted, and on their hops from Terlond to Alland.

But never for such a long trip, putting Zami under. Yanda watched each movement of the elf captain's hand, wanting to know exactly what was done.

Mnenu dropped to his knees and watched Tlalit set up Yanda in her turn. The lid came down. Through the hand-sized window she could see part of Mnenu's face. He smiled at her, then climbed out of sight.

Sound was strange, muffled. An oxygen mask covered her nose and mouth. She heard her breathing loudly. The air coming in seemed fresh enough, with a slight plaz odor. A *psht* announced a light spray and her consciousness slipped away.

Yanda opened her eyes to low lighting. Within seconds the lid on her unit lifted with a *ssh*. She saw Tlalit move away, and others, already up, or climbing out of their beds. Muzzy-headed, she pushed to sitting.

"Wakey-wakey, princess." Mnenu seemed all too bright and cheery for the circumstances. "I'm going to take a quick swim."

"You do that." Yanda stood. Zami was sitting in his open sta-bed. She grabbed him into her arms.

"Just a nap, Mommy." He pressed hands to her collarbone as she squeezed him.

She ruffled his curly hair. "That's right. Just a nap, little trooper. Let's feed you."

She got them set up with hot drink and food in the kitchen and opened her ELAC. She'd left a message for Soni asking how to adjust the pools for greater health.

Merne and Tlalit came in and fixed *kaffe*.

Around a bite of a grain cereal with nuts and fruits, Yanda said, "Shouma wrote me that Sandu has top medical supplies. I wonder if they have reasonable prices on monitoring pools. If you want to fit one on board here, I have access to my funds now from years as a surgeon. I could finance it."

One of Tlalit's eloquent peach brows lifted in an arc. "Sounds practical."

Merne nodded approval. "There's space in a corner of the spa room."

Yanda clapped, thinking of the benefit to Zami and Mnenu as well as Bonden. "It's settled, then?"

Tlalit took up her *kaffe* and headed out the door. "Sounds like it," she called over her shoulder on her way to her lair at the controls.

Yanda hurried to follow. "Are we close to Belsom?"

"Very."

Yanda's stomach churned. Time to make the plan. What would it entail? She was sure she wouldn't be able to see through to Bonden's location from behind a moon. It was too far. She could mind-communicate somewhat at that distance, but see through?

It seemed dangerous to be on Qontaq, though; she'd begun to sense what a warring planet it was. And now, Ilan had disappeared.

She dropped onto a lounge couch, letting Zami crawl to his toys, and sent out a mental message to Shouma. "You at Shamba's Nook?"

"Yes. You're approaching Belsom." Clearly, she was reading arrivals on a screen. Merne must have set her up. In the past, as Yanda had known her all those months sharing captivity on Terlond, Shouma's powers lay in the mind, not in tech.

"So I've been told," Yanda said. "It'll be good to see you in the flesh."

"And you. Look at Zami and let me see him through your eyes."

Yanda encouraged Zami to turn toward her.

Shouma said, into Yanda's mind, "Beautiful boy."

Zami had gotten Tlalit to corn-row part of his hair. The rest hung past his shoulders in wavy curls, magenta at the tips. His ears had taken their elven shape, elongated leaves. One had an earring that shifted color when he wanted. At around three in Allandian years, his facial features had become more defined, only a slight pillow left in the cheeks. His almond skin had begun to show a faint plum undertone.

Over the com system, Tlalit announced: "Please secure yourselves as we enter Belsom's atmosphere. There will be turbulence." She liked to use a formal tone in her captain role.

Yanda moved herself and Zami to benches in the control room, wanting to observe their approach to Belsom. It was a rather golden moon, more than half in shadow. Yanda held Zami's hand as they left the darkness of space and, after a few rugged jolts, shuddered into light that hit the ship at an angle.

Soon a cluster of brightness came into focus. "That must the city of Lantat," Yanda guessed.

"Not much more than a town, really," Tlalit said.

"How does Belsom compare to Prokit's Moon?" Yanda asked, knowing only they were both in the same solar system.

Tlalit's eyes lit up at the mention. "PM has only small towns, but it's rich in culture. Way more than Belsom, which is basically a way-station. Probably because Prok gets more sun. Very sweet sun. Temperatures less extreme."

"Dele is on Prokit's Moon," Yanda mentioned, knowing Tlalit adored the place.

"She's not." Tlalit adjusted a setting on her panel, then peered over her shoulder at Yanda. "Is she?"

"That's what Shouma told me and Vatu."

Tlalit turned back to her controls, lips pressed, with envy, Yanda thought.

The moon grew closer. Where they were headed was dark.

"What time is it there?" Yanda asked Shouma in mind-speak.

"Late." She yawned.

"Sorry to keep you up."

"You think I care? This is exciting."

"Are you close to the spaceport?" Yanda asked.

"I'm close. There are shuttles running. Grab one to Swallow's Lane."

"Okay. Shouldn't be too long."

"I booked you rooms. Several. I hope, enough."

Tlalit was listening in. "We might stay on the ship," she said, into their minds.

Wondering why they wanted to stay onboard, Yanda said only, "You ought to get off. Look around."

Tlalit announced they could get up and move around. Vatu came into the lounge.

"Watch Zami a mo? I'm going to pack a satchel."

"'Course."

A quarter of an hour later, Belsom towers gave permission to land. Mnenu carried the little boy, backpack slung over his shoulder, while Yanda and Vatu followed, making their way down the ramp, off the ship. Light in the distance seemed strangely angled.

"Is that moon or sun?" Yanda hadn't been on a moon that had sun casting across part of it like a constant partial eclipse. The night air smelled faintly of ship fuel amid the sounds of a space port: engines, workers shouting, and the beeping of backing transport vehicles.

Sliding walks with waist-high protective barriers crisscrossed the tarmac from the landing bays. Aqua lights lined guard ropes as they rode away from the *Sarsefi*, then turned green as they made a ninety-degree left turn onto a wider lane approaching buildings.

"I wonder if the shades mean anything," Yanda pondered aloud.

They entered a several-storied, dome-faced edifice through wide auto-doors and found security check-in packed with travelers. *If it's this busy all night, the town must be mostly hotel accommodations and spaceport workers*, Yanda thought.

Shouma had set up VIP check-in for their group. As soon as they gave their names, they were waved through. They followed signs announcing public transport.

"We want Swallows' Lane," Yanda said, scanning the destinations board.

They trooped out to the sidewalk and followed signs to the correct shuttle stop. An open-sided trolly waited, hovering above smooth mauve plaz-paving that exuded a slight artificial odor.

Vatu stepped forward to check the lighted placard on the front. "Yes, this one includes Swallow's Way."

They clambered on. Zami, carried on Yanda's hip 'till they took seats on padded benches, held a lock of Yanda's hair and looked around with his wide swirling eyes. A beanie covered his distinctive ears. They had no real reason to think they should hide their identities at this point yet they took no chances. Vatu had disguised herself and Mnenu. It seemed best to keep a low profile on the tram. Just in case.

The trolly pulled out and whizzed around a traffic circle, passing small and large vehicles as it hummed away from the spaceport. A tree-lined avenue strung with lights turned into a row of single-story shops that turned into a mix with taller buildings.

"This place looks so clean and polished." Vatu's brow, in her typico-human disguise, puckered just slightly with suspicion. "I wonder if there's any crime at all?"

"They're very strict here, actually." Shouma's mind had stayed joined with theirs. "Surveillance everywhere."

"They don't want to be another Shagal, maybe," Yanda muttered in mind-speak, thinking of the moon where a girl like her daughter had first been sighted, a rough port teeming with traffickers, crime, and corruption.

"Maybe it was smart of you to stay on the ship," Yanda thought to Tlalit and Merne back on the *Sarsefi*.

"We'll be set up nice and secure in my room," Shouma assured her.

The vehicle let off a few passengers in front of a multi-story hotel called Cuarto. Yanda took in several star-systems' denizens—one tall narrow being with orange-brown skin wore a hat cocked to one side—before they moved on. Soon they made a right onto Swallows' Way and came to a stop at an inn with flowering vines dotted with fairy lights along a front walk.

Zami's eyes glowed at the sight. "I miss Tuk-Tuk."

Yanda caught a picture in his mind of him running along the entrance to the inn, Tuk-Tuk skitting alongside in the vines, playing chase. She felt bad he didn't have any children to play with on this journey. That would have to be addressed. How long would they be in space, she wondered, not for the first time. Should she have left him with his father in the elven forest where there were children and tiny primates as companions? Not to mention all the benefits of a nursery with elves assigned to teach their ways.

"Should we come to the café or your room first?" Yanda asked, her stomach rumbling at the thought of off-ship food, served hot.

"I'm in my room. There's an all-night restaurant down the block." Shouma gave them the numbers of their rooms.

Mnenu checked them in on his device.

Since they were off the trolly now and alone in the dark, they were safe enough from prying eyes for Yanda to let a map of the inn's maze of cottages pop up holographically above her arm.

The flower-lined walkways smelled sweet, similar to the *wakneet* vine of her childhood. They found their way to five cottages in a row: first was Shouma's. She opened her door and golden light spilled out.

Yanda hurried to the older woman, and they hugged a full minute. Shouma bent to give Zami a peck on the cheek. He smiled, remembering her well from his early life on Terlond.

"Do you want to put your things in your cottage? I picked up hot soup and warm bread for you."

"Oh, you didn't say!" Smelling fresh-baked bread wafting from the interior, Yanda rushed to the neighboring cottage and, using a digital key to let herself and Zami in, dumped their bag on a bed, and turned.

Vatu stood behind her. "Can I stay with you? We could keep separate cottages in case we need space."

"Of course!" Yanda hugged her Mingalean friend, then, holding Zami's hand, headed for Shouma's and food.

They joined Mnenu and Shouma in Room 31. Anticipating the urge for things not readily available on a spaceship, Shouma had laid out a spread: creamy leek soup, freshly baked artisan bread, a mix of brightly colored sauteed veggies, and a few chutneys to add delight. The four newcomers set into the repast as though they'd been starving for weeks.

"You guys should have come." Yanda sent Merne and Tlalit a picture of their feast.

Ten minutes later, a knock came on the door. Tlalit's apricot-peaked head ducked under the lintel, followed by Merne's slightly-less-tall mound of brown-green braids, as the two Elves joined them.

They sat in the two chairs, on beds, or on the rug, plates and bowls perched anywhere they could find space.

Ilan tapped in Yanda's mind. "You've arrived." If anything, he seemed more ragged than ever.

"You're alive!" Yanda straightened up with relief. She sent the news to the rest with her mind and eyes.

"I just had a long sleep. Had to really check out."

"You should have said. We were worried," Yanda chided.

Ilan registered contrition but swiftly moved on. "If you're fresh enough, can we start?"

CHAPTER

5

Everyone had participated in elven mind-power circles. They knew how to form a secure sphere, all around, above and below.

But Shouma pointed out, "This kind of energy doesn't normally involve children. It could be too powerful for Zami's developing mind." She asked Vatu, "Do you want to take Zami to the farthest room?"

Vatu said, "I want to help. I've trained in distance transmogrification. Besides, I think Zami's more than ready." She'd never gotten a chance to sit in the circle of great stone seats in the Vashal crystal pyramid in the elven forest yet had wanted to. She gave Yanda a quick personal message of warmth and friendship, adding, "Not to override you if you feel strongly about it."

"The other option is to have Zami with Chin and the Jejods," Shouma said.

"No, I think Vatu is right. What do you think, Button?" Yanda leaned close to her son.

Zami looked excited. "What will we do?"

Yanda nuzzled his neck. "I'm going on an adventure to save our friend, Bonden. We'll be very good heroes if we can get her out. If you want to sit in the circle, you can help hold the energy." Their eyes met for a moment.

He said, "I want to help," with conviction.

The seven sat on pillows in a ring, against the pushed-apart beds.

"Did you come alone, Shouma?" Yanda asked.

"No, the Jejods and Chin are at a separate location."

"And Beri?" Yanda asked. She'd been hoping to see him.

Mnenu glanced at her, calm but quizzical. She'd told him they weren't lovers. But…Yanda felt a brief flash of jealousy from him.

"Beri couldn't apart from his true love," Shouma reported. "Let's try to get Bonden. If we need a stronger circle, we can bring Aktat and the others here quickly. There're just down the street."

Ilan waited, silent, through this exchange. Now he said, "Let's see what we can do."

"What's the plan?" Shouma asked.

He outlined, "I studied the guards at the SG. Picked one. About my size. I'll 'become' him and channel Yanda. Basically, she'll be in spirit-travel, in me. If you're up for that, Yanda."

"That's how I'll get my sight close without having to go onto Qontaq. Good idea." Yanda had never literally gone into another but imagined it would be similar to mind-meld.

Shouma said, "We can amplify Yanda's ability to see-through in order to get a look at the entire facility and find Bonden."

"Exactly," Ilan said. "Can we try it?"

"How do we get her out once we find her?" Yanda asked. "Is a medical ship going to be there to get her to care on Sandu, Shouma?" Yanda asked.

"My son has one waiting here on Belsom," Shouma assured them. "We didn't want to have trouble leaving Qontaq."

"Merne can hop there and bring them back here," Yanda said. "She's gone from Terlond to Alland and brought Zami with her so, shouldn't be too hard from here." A little acerbic. She'd never fully forgiven Merne for bringing her son across space without consulting her.

"That's true." Mnenu glanced from Merne to Yanda. He knew they'd never really hashed that out and would eventually have to.

Merne and Yanda locked eyes. Merne's dropped away first.

"Can we clear the air of this before starting a very intense operation?" Shouma asked.

Merne got up and came across the circle to drop cross-legged in front of Yanda. Hands on her arms, she pressed her forehead to Yanda's and gave her a heartfelt apology. Pulling her head back, her swirling eyes penetrated into Yanda's. "I understand how that must have felt. I wanted to surprise you but I see that it left you feeling powerless, losing trust, wondering what else I might do without speaking with you first."

Tears pricked in Yanda's eyes. She leaned forward, sitting up straight but not reaching the other's height. "You will in future ask me?"

Merne nodded, eyes swirling. "I will, little sister."

Yanda nodded and Merne returned to sit opposite her,

between Tlalit and Shouma. Yanda took Zami's hand on one side, Vatu on the other.

The Circle created a secure sphere, the air crackling with electricity. Zami adeptly lent his energy to the whole. Yanda breathed in, settling into the pillows behind her, readying.

Ilan pulled on her spirit. They felt the bond they'd formed on Alland while traveling to the rebel camp. Her spirit slipped easily into his mind.

Zami felt his mother's body go limp against the pillows piled behind her. Stomach churning, he peered at her slack face and edged closer, curling into her side. He kept hold of her hand, but wedged his shoulder in under her arm. Welded into the Circle's mind-meld, he stayed with her spirit, gripping with all his heart.

Yanda looked out from Ilan's eyes. She realized spirit travel was a fuller experience than just sharing minds. She'd spirit-traveled with Zamani and Tenali and felt herself in the sea with them, but had never gone into another's mind. Her thoughts blended with his.

She looked around at a dingy, spare room. Gray light seeped through thin curtains, leaving the rented accommodation mostly dark.

Ilan eased out of a scarred, creaky chair and headed down a narrow staircase.

They reached a dismal alley as shadowed as the hotel room. Yanda perceived Ilan's mental register shifting. They left the alley, turning onto a larger street. It seemed to be a warehouse district, dotted here and there with convenience stores and squalid cafés.

They approached a plain gray edifice that conveyed a military air. It was surrounded by high fences with warning signs of electric wires on top.

"I studied the guards over a number of days, chose one, and hacked his codes." Ilan showed her a mental picture of the guy similar to Ilan in size. Then Yanda caught Ilan's reflection in a plaz window. It didn't look like him. This was a dark-haired man wearing a cap and uniform, a one-piece gray coverall, with the SG insignia in red.

"What's SG?" she asked.

"It's a research facility. Tied to the military. Supposed to relate to medical research." He snorted.

They crossed an entry lane and followed the fence to an employee entrance.

First test. He'd created a card with the correct codes keyed in, he explained as he slid it through.

They were on the grounds. So far so good.

"What happened to you the first times you tried?" Yanda asked. "You seem…" weak she thought but hid that idea. "…are you injured?"

The first, main, sprawling building had several wings of bare gray institutional exterior. The central part was ten or so stories, that Yanda could see.

Ilan stood in the dark for a moment, studying. And not answering her question. "I'm not sensing her here."

Yanda agreed. "But isn't she blocked from—"

"I know, but I have a search-bot running her register."

They skirted the largest edifice. At the back, a five-story building stretched the length of the yard. A sign read, Level Four Security.

Yanda felt something familiar. She said into the mind-meld, "Can everyone amplify sensing Bonden's mind? She might be sleeping or...incapacitated."

Ilan stopped.

"I feel her, too." Yanda could see through the outside wall but no farther. "Help me push my reach," she requested of the powerful group-mind.

Like an onion unfolding, she saw the building in layers, some overlapping. Walls, floors, hallways, up through the levels.

There was only one room she could not penetrate even with the power of their group amplifying her sight.

"That must be the cell," she thought. It was about eight-by-eight feet embedded past several foyers, entered through thick security doors.

Ilan strode toward the entrance and pressed his simulated ID to the panel. A red triangle blinked. "Not approved personnel," read the screen.

Yanda couldn't tell if her own heart was hammering or only Ilan's. The pulse in his neck and rush of blood to his vital organs seemed like her own yet were far more volatile. *What if this sets off alarms*?!

Ilan moaned. "I thought this guy had higher clearance." He darted around the side of the building and into a recessed area at the back, fearing the whole place would be alerted to an attempted entry.

He crouched against a rough stucco wall, boots gritting on gravel and stone, listening, heart hammering. Then he pulled a device from a pocket in the thick vest that was part of the uniform. Hunching over, he tapped.

"Is this what you encountered before?" Yanda asked.

"She wasn't in this building. She's been moved. This kind of thing, yeah. I thought I had it right this time."

"You're here," Bonden whispered in their minds, faint.

Relief rushed through Yanda.

Ilan blew a gust of air. "We're here. I have the wrong ID." He hated admitting that, Yanda could tell.

"The assholes in here probably don't show up in the system. There's one named Phanic." Though she registered as very weak, she managed to give them a picture of his appearance: black greasy hair, piercings, a uniform entirely different from the assigned beige SG one-piece coverall.

"Can you give us a mental register?" Ilan didn't know if Bonden could do this, let alone pass it on. Not many could. It was an unusual power.

"I'll try next time he comes. He's a prick," Bonden said, voice faint.

"Wonderful." Ilan drew it out with dark sarcasm.

"He'll be bringing food." Bonden said weakly.

"We have to watch what kind of ID he uses," Yanda said.

"Thanks to you, we can at least see what he does," Ilan said.

"Now that we have the location, I'm keying in on the security systems." Merne tapped away at her keyboard. "I see him."

"I do, too," Shouma said. "I'm going to send him away. He'll remember an errand. Then you'll have a window of time. He seems to be the only one in the building."

"Before you do, please have him leave his ID tag behind," Tlalit said.

Relief flooded Yanda, to know Tlalit and Merne were on this part.

"I've got the tech security throughout the building," Merne said. "Ilan, you can help me scrub after, removing the history of this, but for now I'll turn off the camera feeds."

Ilan moved stealthily to a side entrance where Shouma directed him to watch for Phanic's exit. The slope-shoul-dered man slinked out the door and moved off toward the perpendicular row of buildings. Ilan caught the door as the guard disappeared from sight. Gaining the top level easily with security shut off, Ilan arrived at the wall of ominous black onyx where Bonden was kept. A security badge lay on a side table. Ilan picked it up and pressed the oval code to a panel, making the windowless door open.

He was through the first layer. A cold featureless ves-tibule held a second door. Ilan stepped to it, tried the ID badge, immediately realized it was an optic plate in the center of the door. "This one requires his retina," Ilan said, in a low growl of frustration.

The web of minds on Belsom hopped with Shouma to Phanic on Qontaq. Invisible, she stared at his eyes like a camera as he waited for *kaffe* at a machine.

"Got it," Tlalit and Merne both said at once and con-veyed the eye-print to Ilan. He assimilated this information to his facsimile of Phanic and pressed his eye to the clear plaz to be read.

The lock snapped. He shoved open the door, sending a message to Bonden. There was a third door, thick as a bank vault, Yanda thought, peering through it, but there was Bonden, lying on a filthy pallet, looking more dead than alive.

"*Akrat*," Ilan swore. "This one requires thumb print." With a sigh, he shoved his thumb with little hope. The smaller man's digit immediately registered and Ilan practically fell into the cell in his surprise. "I guess I got that detail of the replica correct."

"Couldn't Shouma have just jumped in there, like she got in with Phanic just now?" Mnenu asked reasonably.

"It's blocked against psi, remember? Or Bonden could have walked out through the wall." Ilan knelt by his fellow Qontaqian. "Bonden?" He shook her shoulder. No response. "Shouma, can you bring us if I get her outside of this ghastly hell-hole?"

Ilan transformed to himself in order to have the strength to carry the stocky inventor out of the torture chamber into the hallway, easily exiting through the other two thick doors.

Clasping hands tighter, the Circle went to their highest place of power, but could not lift both Ilan and Bonden out of the building, much less to Belsom.

"I'll get the Jejods and Chin," Shouma said.

CHAPTER

6

With Merne and Tlalit holding off security—agitating that there would be a timer on it and probably soon an alarm would be set off—Yanda took over Phanic's mind. Shouma had taught them enough to control a non-psi in simple ways.

Vatu helped by transforming herself into a Qontaqian female to distract Phanic. She'd taken an image from his mind of the type of woman he likes: alternative, with chains on a faux-leather jacket, tats, hair magenta frizz-loops, she sauntered down the hall and leaned against the machine where Phanic sipped his drink.

"You new?" he asked.

"Yeah, night shift. Sucks." In grabbing an identity, Vatu also imprinted the mental register and could use the Qontaqian version of universal language fluently.

Meanwhile, Shouma used her flagging energy to travel instantly to the hotel more suited to very tall exo-beings, with exercise trees in a hall three stories high, and brought Chin back. The Jejods preferred to run.

Chin, large with soldier's build and stance, strode in in canvas jacket, all-terrain khakis and boots the size of anvils. She took her usual wide-legged stance, hair shooting up in a short butch, awaiting direction.

Through the eyes of the hivemind, Yanda watched Chin arrive and longed to be there. "I think my energy would will be more valuable on Belsom. Can you bring me back? I'm not needed to see through anymore."

The group withdrew her spirit. Returning consciousness to her body, she opened her eyes.

Zami, monitoring her face, leaped into her lap and pressed himself to her.

Yanda wrapped her arms around him. "I'm here, Button. Thank you for letting me do that." She nuzzled his neck. He clung to her.

Seconds later, the Jejods raced in their long bird stride to Room 31. The three gangly sisters ducked under the doorsill, Aktat, the eldest, then Jat, and finally the youngest, Tik. Inside, they kept their feathered heads stooped to miss the ceiling. Dark martial clothing belted snugly around them emphasized their long thin forms. Like Chin's clothing, straps held unknown tools. Rubbery boots showed each toe of their long curving feet, reminding Yanda of the material that composed the mountainsides of their world.

Beds pushed back, they folded into the expanded circle. As the hivemind formed, all saw Ilan holding Bonden.

Vatu called into their minds, "Phanic's on his way."

Merne watched on the surveillance screens as he mounted the last stairs to Bonden's floor.

The circle built their power together, energy swelling, and pulled Ilan to them. He appeared in the hotel room, at the center of their circle, holding the unconscious Bonden. He stepped to a bed and laid her down. She was a substantial woman, built stocky. Still, she didn't wake.

"We need to get out of here." Ilan sat on the edge of the bed and stroked Bonden's arm which had welts and deep multi-colored bruises, blue, yellow, purple, showing stages of healing, or brand new.

Bonden suddenly thrashed. "I won't!" she cried.

Ilan stroked her forehead, brushing back sweat-soaked hair. "It's okay. You're safe now."

Yanda glanced around at the others. "She's talking to her captors? What did they want her to do?"

Ilan said, "That's why she was tortured. They wanted her to use her powers for them." He leaned toward her to hear anything else she said, but her mouth dropped slack again, her swollen eyes never opening.

"Ship?" Ilan pleaded.

Shouma said, "Tedro's has emergency supports. Might be safest to get her to Sandu."

"Let's do it." Ilan straightened, impatient.

Shouma, strength waning, brought Bonden with her to the Sandu medical supply ship.

When she was gone, Tlalit said, "Alarms have gone off and a search has been initiated."

"I'm a wanted man." Ilan rubbed his red-gold stubbly cheeks wearily.

"Come on. Let's gather our stuff." Yanda, carrying Zami, hurried next door for her bag. Vatu followed while the Jejods raced to their hotel and back again, bringing with them their totes and Chin's.

"I guess we're riding the normal way," Ilan said.

Vatu offered, "For this short distance, I can disguise everyone."

A work crew was decided on. It would draw the least attention arriving at the base port.

Yanda and the rest wore tool belts and badges matching the Belsom spaceport. Despite the time—in the wee hours of the morning—several travelers were already on the conveyance. These passengers took no notice of them. Yanda thought Zami liked getting to be a grown-up, in body and even persona. He stood tall, and she read excitement in his mind, but it was odd for her to see him that way. She'd be happy to see him a child again.

Instead of making their way straight to the *Sarsefi*, they walked around the side of the main port building toward a hanger. Disbursing, they found ways into the shadows and took back routes to the *Sarsefi*. Merne and Tlalit hurried ahead onto the ship and changed nearby surveillance cameras to old vid feeds just in case. Each of them entered the ship one at a time by an entrance facing away from surveillance. Once on the ship, Vatu shifted each back to their natural form.

Ilan looked around, his usual self in appearance. He was clearly agitated over Bonden.

Yanda gave him a tour while Vatu showed the Jejods and Chin the sleeping quarters. When everyone had gathered back in the common area, they decided the Jejods could stay in the hall next door where ceilings were higher and Tlalit had installed exercise bars. Vatu and Yanda would share so Ilan and Chin could have rooms.

Mnenu hurried around, checking settings, making the ship ready for takeoff, keeping contact with Tlalit in the control room with a comm unit on his wrist.

Yanda called to him in mind-speak, "Did they get fuel?"

"Yeah, before they came to the room they had all the supplies we needed delivered," he responded.

"*Sarsefi* preparing to depart from Belsom port," Tlalit announced into her mic.

The ten passengers strapped in along walls of the main lounge and control room.

They listened to Tlalit grumbling that Belsom's security usually went smoothly, being a place of frequent transit; flight regulators seemed to rest easy in the knowledge that, on the moon's surface, safety was regulated for a clean tourist-friendly environment. But flight administration had been warned of two wanted Qontaqians. She put the official on speaker for all to hear.

"We need a manifest of your travelers," said the robotic flight regulator.

"Certainly." Tlalit sent him the same list they had on arrival.

Predicting this possibility, Merne had set body heat imprints to zero for the additional passengers so they would not be read by any system.

"Is there a problem?" Tlalit asked innocently.

"Well, there's been some sort of government breach down on Qontaq. High security. But no way they could have gotten onto our moon this quickly. You're free to go."

Puffing a relieved breath, Tlalit tapped in settings. "Thank you." She shut off the connection. A bead of sweat ran down her temple, revealing the intensity of the moment, even for the unflappable elf.

Anti-grav pulled at their bodies as they lifted off. Sounds of grinding, wind resistance, and the whining of instrumentation accompanied a whiff of liquid hydrogen burn-off.

Yanda pulled masks from a chair arm compartment and slipped over her mouth and nose, another over Zami's. Mnenu, beside her, took her hand.

Yanda saw Ilan looking at their held-hands from his wide seat on the far wall. His gaze lifted to her face. There were dark bags under his eyes in layered pockets.

"You should rest your head back, try to sleep," she said in mind-speak, just to him.

She was aware of Mnenu glancing from her to Ilan and felt slight irritation. "Is this going to be weird?" she asked herself. Not that there'd been anything between her and Ilan. She'd told Mnenu that. The tensions between the men seemed never-ending. Something about her powers. An energy. Much as she hated the competition, she wanted Ilan on this trip, hoped he'd stay. The power he held livened dormant parts of her.

Others had had effects on her. What would she call it? Magic? She suspected Ilan helped awaken her burgeoning AI understanding. Mnenu brought forth her ability to transform to a sea creature—*lanten*. Shouma had taught her to extend her reach, not just with sight but with telepathy. It was more than teaching. Different triggers had been catalysts. What more was in her?

The air grew electric before they transited out of Belsom's atmosphere. Pressure pushed against Yanda. She sank into her seat, head back, breath shallow.

They floated in blackness in a sphere of stars. When the announcement came that they could move around freely, Yanda unbuckled herself, then Zami. He slid onto his knees to play on the rug. Yanda rumpled his hair. They hadn't had a chance to talk about any of these experiences. She wanted to check in with him. There would be time, she told herself.

Chin and the Jejods came out of the control room.

"I'm going to bring refreshments." Merne left for the kitchen.

Tlalit stretched in the doorway, arms pressed over her head. "Where to?"

"Let's check on Bonden, then figure it out?" Yanda suggested. They hive-minded, connecting to Shouma. "Did you get away okay?"

"I brought Bonden onto the *Lilanca*, her energy imprint disguised," Shouma said. "This ship has strong security — layers of it — used to conduct clandestine emergency operations when fighting factions are involved."

"How's Bonden?" Chin sat on the floor against the wall, muscular arms hugging her knees. She'd been close to Bonden in their captivity together, fond of the quiet tinkerer with a brusque manner like her own.

"She's in a monitoring bed," Shouma told them, "getting what she needs medically. But she has brutal injuries. Might have a ruptured spleen. I'm not sure what else. Probably much beyond the physical. I'll give you an update as soon as I can. I've told Chela to be waiting."

Merne said, in mind-speak to those on both ships, "But do you think it's safe to take her to a hospital? Ilan's wanted and so's she."

"Maybe not. I'll ask my son about a secure location." Shouma left and came back. "There's a satellite. He says we can pretty much disappear there. Tlalit, I'll have him give you coordinates."

"We can disappear best on Erzon," Aktat said, perched

next to her sisters on the exercise bars. "Part of our planet is always cloudy. The gases throw instruments off."

"That's a thought," Merne replied.

"This satellite seems closest. Will we meet there?" Tlalit asked.

Shouma suddenly cried out to them. "They're losing her. Bonden's not responding!"

"We need the Flari," Yanda said.

"What's that?" several asked.

"A healing pool." Yanda explained the pool Soni had used on her and Zami in Pedore on her home planet. "Shouma, are there any Flaris on Sandu?"

Shouma was silent a moment, communicating out of range of the hivemind. "My son can get one sent. We've got another problem."

"What?" Tlalit asked, voice tense.

"Bonden must have a powerful sensor embedded in her. They've detected her, even on this protected ship. They're following us."

Sharing Shouma's sight, Yanda and the others saw Bonden's face through the clear cover of the healing bed: ashen, drawn, bruised, eyes closed and sunken.

"Shouldn't you be in stasis, Shouma?" Tlalit asked.

The *Sarsefi* was coasting, waiting for a final word on the destination.

"Let's trade her onto my ship," Tlalit said. "I can 'disappear' her."

"She's slipping from us." Shouma had never sounded so bleak.

"I can get to Erzon if we can rendezvous and transfer her," Tlalit urged.

Yanda dropped to the carpet next to Zami and pulled

him into her lap, to ground herself as well as him.

Aware of the tension, Zami brought his whirling eyes to Yanda's. "We'll help her."

She felt it as a statement, felt her son's confidence. "Yes, we will." Yanda squeezed him, then swung him onto her hip as she strode into the control room. "Let's get our heads in gear," she said to the whole group, stretched across light years. "Best way to get the Flari Regeneration Bath to us. Best way to hide Bonden. Quickest way to disappear and heal her."

Vatu came in behind her. Mnenu was at the panels next to Tlalit. Merne entered from the kitchen toting a tray of snacks. The Jejod sisters stalked in, bending their heads only slightly since the control room entrance was built tall for Elves.

"Oh-kay. Here's how we do it," Aktat said. The bird-like sisters fanned out around the controls. "It's just as fast for Tedro to bring the *Lilanca* into the clouds, hyperdrive. We rendezvous there." She explained the detection method to keep the panels adjusted for the location she had in mind in the gaseous section of Erzon.

Maps appeared on air-screens. Jat sat down at a keyboard. Swift calculations ran in streams across displays.

CHAPTER

7

Three small space vessels had to be timed precisely for rendezvous in Erzon's gaseous region.

"This is weird to navigate," Tlalit stressed as they sank into clouds, approaching a floating city that registered on the screen but was invisible to their naked eyes.

All watched as the readings showed another ship.

"It's Shouma's son's," Tlalit assured them.

"I'm surprised he approved this excursion, with the Qontaqian government at our heels," Yanda said.

Shouma said, "They respond to all kinds of emergencies."

"Has Bonden come to yet?" Yanda asked her.

"No. But we're in luck regarding your Flari. It's uncommon to even know about the highly specialized pools, but the medical research facility on Sandu has experimented with them. They're a very sophisticated establishment."

"Is there one on hand?" Yanda asked, not terribly hopeful.

"As a matter of fact, there is," Shouma said. We've commandeered another of Sandu's medical tech ships to bring it."

On her ENAC, Yanda sent an encrypted message to Soni on Alland. They'd need her advice on the Flari settings. "I can't get a signal out," she said, low-voiced, to Ilan. They were seated in the lounge. Most of the others remained crowded in there or the control room. Gravity was off-kilter in the rest of the ship and things occasionally went flying through the air. Better to stay in a room where seats were attached to walls; they'd closed Zami's toy cupboard and anything else had been shoved into drawers. Zami played with Tik and Vatu, using low-grav to bounce out of reach.

"Let me see." Ilan tapped swiftly on his device, programming lines of code.

Ilan took one of Yanda's hands. "Give me a picture."

Yanda thought about Soni, the brilliant, androgynous health tech in the underground refuge of Pedore. With Ilan's immense energy enhancing her reach, she sensed the woman look up, gaze around. Then their minds clicked together despite the interference of Erzonian atmosphere.

"Soni, this is Yanda." She reminded the other woman of her stay at Pedore, how Soni had helped Yanda and her son Zami in the healing pools.

"Greetings," Soni said brightly. "There's an odd static around you."

"Yes, we're in a strange cloud place. Ilan is helping me reach you. He was one of those who helped me on Alland after I left Pedore."

"Haven't I met you?" Soni asked Ilan. "With Jelat one time?"

"That's true. Your mind reminds me of a Qontaqian," Ilan said.

A jealous twinge in Yanda's gut took her by surprise.

"I do have Qontaqian blood." Soni admitted surprise at his perception since she'd spent most of her life on Alland.

"We have a very sick, wounded friend," Yanda went on. "Also Qontaqian." Why were so many Qontaqians amazing? she asked herself silently, then said with urgency, "Bonden's slipping away. She's so…so dear to us. *And* so talented. We have a Flari pool coming and would appreciate your guidance."

"Wow. That's really tense." Soni's mind conveyed worry. "I want to help. This feels hard, though. Our connection is hurting my head."

"Oh, no." Yanda turned to Ilan and whispered, "Maybe we have to bring her here?"

"Would you be willing to come to us?" Ilan asked Soni. "I don't think your head will hurt once here. Ours don't."

"Sure, I'll come." Soni's mind swirled with questions. She had never hopped across space.

Yanda admired her willingness to jump off into the unknown. She also had to wonder about her seeming eagerness to leave Alland.

Soni added, "I'm insane, right?"

"You're compassionate," Ilan said. "And Bonden's worth it."

Yanda brought Merne and Shouma into their mindmeld. "Can you bring Soni here? We're going to need her.

She's an expert on the Flari. But mind-meld with us here on Erzon is hurting her head. She's said she'll come."

"I designed it." Soni's tone was modest.

"Wow." Merne was impressed. "Give us her mind-print. She's on Alland?"

Yanda affirmed. She and Ilan had moved to the rug, giving up their seats to others. Merne joined them, backs against the wall. Bodies touching was much more power-ful. They sent a mental request to the rest to help. As much as possible, the others put a hand on each other or pressed against someone, clustering in the lounge. Tlalit helped, keeping part of her mind on the controls as she stared out at clouds. Zami climbed into Yanda's lap.

As one mind, they entered the space around Soni. The youngish woman with long, dark-red braids, closed her eyes, swaying with the sudden impact of their minds in hers. Yanda felt her startled, awed reaction, overwhelmed but also valuing the moment. Soni took deep breaths.

Shouma, the natural teacher, said to her, "We're going to bring you with us. Try to relax into it."

Yanda wondered if that was what Merne had said to Zami when she fetched him from her home world without her permission, and brought him to Terlond where she worked with the sea elves to find her daughter. Merne had wanted to surprise her. It would have taken weeks to bring him by ship, and Merne knew Yanda wanted to search for Seiti quickly, following a vision of her in Unknown Space. It was a good surprise. It still tested Yanda's trust of Merne, that she'd take her son across space without their discuss-ing it, added to her worry that in the end, Zamani would want to keep her son in the elven forest. She held Zami tight as they both helped with the transport.

In an instant, Soni stood in their midst on the ship—elves, bird-like Jejods, a small Mingalean shapeshifter... Only she and Ilan were familiar to Soni.

Pressing her hands to her face, light freckles standing out, Soni took deep breaths, then smiled shyly as her hands came away.

Still in her mind, Yanda saw her take in the view through the doorway to the control room, of oddly-colored roiling clouds. Yanda jumped up to hug Soni. "Thank you for coming to us."

Soni hugged her back, a faint flush in her cheeks. She tried to walk toward the cloud-view and found her steps bounding with low *grav*. She laughed, self-conscious, grabbing the doorjamb. In the control room, she stared through the viewing windows. Others followed, bouncing also.

"There are always storms in some pockets," Aktat explained, head bent, gazing out.

"You're from here?" Soni asked the gangly bird-woman next to her.

Aktat nodded. Introductions began and took a while.

Ilan unfolded from the carpet and came to tower over Soni near the controls. "I thank you as well." He put a large hand on her slight shoulder. "It's a big sacrifice."

Soni shrugged. "I'm a healer."

He smiled, then asked Tlalit, "Have you had word?"

Merne, sitting next to her captain-partner, brought up a 3D screen above the panels. "There." She pointed. Nothing appeared where she indicated except a slight disturbance, like a rift, a tear. "This screen detects changes in atmospheric matter. That's Tedro's ship, and there's another Sandu vessel behind."

"Are they headed this way?" Yanda pressed closer to

peer at the grid in the air, barely readable to her untrained eye.

"They're approaching." Mnenu had been watching the trajectory of the minor disturbance.

The *Sarsefi* drew toward a mass of light that Yanda guessed was a city. Pulses of energy glowed in and out on the screen.

"Is anyone following them?" Tik asked, head arcing over the group toward specs of texture on black.

"I've detected no pursuit since we entered the Erzon haze." Merne tapped at her keyboard every few seconds.

Yanda read in Shouma's mind that Tedro's Lilanca drew closer. "Is that the ship with the Flari, following you?" she asked her old friend, still close from their long captivity together.

A male voice came over the speaker, "Lilanca calling the *Sarsefi*."

"I've identified you," Tlalit responded. "I'm going to pull you gently and lock onto you."

Soon the ships clanged, the impact throwing the passengers nearly off their feet.

"Sorry. That would normally be smoother," Shouma's son spoke again.

"Opening the first doors," Tlalit announced.

Yanda carried Zami as she and the rest hurried toward the lower deck. Mnenu put on helmet and suit to enter the low-oxygen entry chamber. Though the Jejods could breathe here, no one knew yet what the others' reactions would be to the atmosphere. A few waited in the vestibule. The rest backed into the hall to make space.

Bonden floated in, encased on a stretcher, hooked up to tubes and monitors with one of Lilanca crew guiding from behind. Ilan grabbed the end as gravity took hold.

They proceeded to the cargo elevator to rise the two floors up where the spa room would hold the Flari.

Shouma and Chela trailed in space suits. Yanda hugged their puffy apparel, unsure whether to follow the stretcher or stay. She decided to stay.

The *Sarsefi* shook as the Lilanca detached. In moments, another ship attached to the entry chute with a bump. Doors *shiffed* open and space-suited crew carried in a large box. Merne led them to the cargo lift.

Yanda could see Chela's familiar face through her visor. Chela, the warm-hearted healer who'd delivered Zami and been a nanny to him at times through their months of captivity. Chela's eyes widened to see her, Zami in her arms.

Shouma lifted off her helmet. "I have to return to my granddaughter. It was so good to see you again, even briefly. Here and on Belsom. You must visit me when you've found your daughter."

Yanda's throat tightened. The elder woman sounded sure. Yanda felt anything but.

The Sandu delivery workers returned from delivering the large box. The three hugged again and Shouma reluctantly left with the Lilanca crew.

Chela stripped off her suit. Yanda stowed it, then led the way to the elevator. As it rose, they gazed at each other. What to say, after they'd been through so much together, then parted for many months. Chela put her arms out to Zami. He climbed eagerly into her embrace and rested his head on her shoulder.

"I've missed you, my sweet." She kissed his cheek and he smiled, shy, a bit puzzled but content.

The elevator door slid open and they hurried into the pool room, Yanda in the lead.

In one corner, Soni worked with Ilan to set up the Flari. The pool was nearly as tall as her. Lights glowed bright blue from within as it filled.

Chela handed Zami to Yanda with a kiss on the cheek and rushed to Bonden's side. Chela and Bonden had perhaps formed the closest connection of anyone in the Citadel on Terlond, where spy mages monitored the ten fem captives day and night in their single long room with its rows of beds. The two quiet women had spent endless hours together, Bonden tinkering, Chela mending clothes or blending herbs.

Soni adeptly replaced tubes with specialized Flari connections. An upright apparatus hummed, dials glowing. Bonden looked worse than ever, hardly alive. Tears coursed down Chela's cheeks as she stood near Soni, watching and asking questions. Soni murmured answers as she adjusted settings. She gently lifted Bonden's eyelids, one at a time, let them drop.

Chela touched Bonden's sallow, bruised face, took one cold hand in hers.

When the Flari tub was nearly full of ultraviolet water, shining up on Soni's face, she pronounced it ready. Merne and Tlalit rigged privacy panels around the corner. Chela and Soni undressed Bonden. Ilan and Chin lifted her into the pool, Soni guiding a single drip-line attached to Bonden's arm as they lowered her into the warm water that coursed and bubbled on the surface.

Soni concentrated on the settings, monitoring levels, reading Bonden's needs. She frowned. "I'm not understanding everything, even with the X-rays forwarded by Tlalit from the Lilanca." She turned to Yanda.

Chela gently pushed Yanda forward. "Yes, use your sight. See what's happening inside her."

Standing on a step that ran around the base of the pool, Yanda reached over the side and rested a hand on Bonden's shoulder, submerged in the warm bluish waters. Her inner sight gazed down through the layers of her body—flesh, sinew, veins, bone, tissues. She winced at the many injuries as she searched the length of her. Surface ones were healing but organs were damaged.

Minutes went by. She could not identify what threatened Bonden's life as her friend's body came closer and closer to shutting down. Catching Soni's eye, she shook her head.

"I'd like to submerge her fully," Soni mumbled half to herself, as though such a thing were impossible. "Head, too."

"Hook her up to an oxygen tank?" Yanda suggested.

Mnenu stepped to the side of the Flari. "If you go *lanten*, you can breathe for Bonden underwater so the Flari can get to all of her. Get in with her."

The Flari was wide enough, Yanda thought. She glanced around at the others, questioning. "I'm not sure." She turned to Soni. "The settings for Bonden might...wrongly affect me, don't you think?"

Soni frowned in thought. "Let me change something." She slid a knob up and lowered another. "That should be okay."

"I don't know if this will help." Yanda stripped off her overalls, designed by Elves, stretchy, from natural mushroom and lichen fibers—the next best thing to wearing nothing. She climbed the steps and crouched at the top, then gingerly crept in next to the other woman, unconscious of her nakedness as she thought only of helping Bonden.

At the touch of the saline mixture, Yanda went *lanten*, her bones becoming more malleable, skin like that of a dolphin, eyes larger and luminous. Gills opened on her sides. She edged up to the unconscious Bonden and wrapped her arms around her, putting her mouth pressed to hers as they submerged.

They remained in the warm glowing waters, Yanda's arms wrapped around the still-inert Bonden.

Mnenu watched Yanda slip off the cream-colored overalls she wore most of the time on the ship. He admired her golden body, remembering how it felt to make love to her.

His breaths came quicker as Yanda transformed to *lanten*. It felt right that she should go *lanten* for this. He had some sense that instincts increase with the change to sea creature.

He shook himself, back to the urgency of the moment, and said to Soni, "Can the intravenous be removed now?"

She hesitated, then nodded and slipped the needle from Bonden's arm, allowing the two women to sink deeper.

Vatu touched Mnenu, and the two moved as one toward the long lap pool, becoming *lanten* the instant they dove in. They joined minds with Yanda, saw what she saw, sensed what she sensed.

CHAPTER

8

Yanda hardly thought with her conscious mind as she searched within Bonden for the underlying cause of the woman's deteriorating state. As moments ticked by, a subtle knowledge seeped in, more native, more instinctual. At the very back of her mind, she was aware when Mnenu and Vatu took *lanten* state in the other pool, and when Zami asked to join them. He swam deep, easily shifting, naturally taking his sea form in the pool filled with Terlond ocean water.

Yanda perceived darkness, as though the lights were turned low. She could have been deep under the sea, instincts leading her energies.

Then others were present, not from the ship. Where were they? Erzon?

"Yandawi," a woman's voice intoned.

Yanda started at the name and the voice, both familiar and foreign.

"Daughter, why not use your powers? You can heal

anything that's willing to be healed."

Daughter? No. She couldn't bear the pain of being tempted to believe her mother reached out to her. What was happening? Maybe it was due to the bath being set for a severely wounded woman. Could it precipitate a fracturing of the mind? The waters running through her gills were designed for a different body—what might they do to her?

But would Soni endanger her health? Not likely. What did the voice mean, "you can heal anything willing to be healed"?

"Ask her." The voice came again, and it was dear to her, yet harsh, demanding, expectant.

Ask her? Ask Bonden? She took the mind-meld deeper. "How do I heal you?" She was in Bonden's subconscious now, speaking to parts of her that the injured woman could not consciously access.

Bonden's deep-self told her, "They tried to find the source of my powers. Injured that part of me."

Mnenu, Vatu, Zami and the rest on board the *Sarsefi* heard.

"They tried to reach where powers dwell, where instinct and intellect blend."

That was the message they all got from Bonden.

Was that where her powers merged? Yanda wondered. Still feeding the other woman oxygen, Yanda drifted so far into Bonden's unconscious, she started to lose her sense of self. Alarms went off as her mind became lost and confused.

Rugged hands pulled at her. "Yanda!"

Vaguely she sensed Ilan's large strong hands tugging at her.

Vatu leapt into the Flari and took over breathing for Bonden as Ilan roughly hauled Yanda from the healing tub.

He shouted her name again, calling her back. In his broad arms, *lanten* left Yanda. She went limp and began shaking. Her lids opened. Ilan's worried eyes peered at her face. In a dazed fog, she took in his angry, worried expression.

"Do you know how dangerous that is?" His voice broke. "Let others help, too." He sounded rough, irritated but his lower lip trembled. He pressed it in tight, bit it to control it.

As her shaking increased, Mnenu, still wet from the lap pool, pulled her from Ilan's arms. "You might need to go *lanten* again. It could ease the shock."

After a brief tussle, Ilan holding on, Yanda landed on her feet, wobbly and shivering.

"That abrupt breaking from it…" Mnenu insisted.

"I…think I'm okay." Yanda edged toward Ilan, questioning.

Pulling on AI, he remained in Bonden's unconscious mind. Holding his arm, Yanda followed his thoughts as he searched for the location of the woman's injured powers. He gripped the rounded foot of the tub. "I think I have an answer," Ilan mumbled.

A frisson shivered through Yanda and the rest whose minds were still joined. She saw Bonden's head come up out of the water. She scooted to the seat built into the head of the tub, eyes finally open.

Yanda sucked in a breath. "Bonden! You're awake."

She glanced at Soni, who quickly attached monitors, fingers shaking at the woman's sudden seeming recovery.

Vatu stood up in the tall-sided tub, unsure what to do. Her outfit that transformed with her in *lanten* looked like the old picture books of mermaids.

Soni's eyes widened as she took in the readings. "She's better. Much better."

Bonden said, "I feel a bit more myself. Tired but..."

"You probably need food," Chela suggested. "Why don't I—"

Soni broke in. "I'll put in new settings. It would be best for you to stay in the water for the recovery phase. But you've regained—" she shook her head— "so much body function."

Vatu scrambled out of the Flari as cries of joy went up throughout the ship. Clapping, hoots and whistles filled the spa room.

Suddenly Bonden's cheeks flushed with a pinprick of color. Her eye sockets seemed less dark and sunken. She willingly laid back into Soni's hands as the younger woman guided her to the headrest, leaving minimal monitors attached. Yanda leaned over the side and touched Bonden's face, tears filming her sight.

Bonden grabbed at her hand. "Thank you," she said, voice husky with emotion.

Chela headed for the door with Merne, discussing what food would be best.

"Soothing soup," Soni called after them.

Yanda stood at the side of the pool, shivering, lost in a multitude of emotions that burbled up in waves: Bonden recovered, her familiar team together on the *Sarsefi*, so long lost to her. She had missed them achingly. The thought coursed from various parts of the ship through their shared hive-mind.

Mnenu held out her coveralls to her. "You're shivering. You should dry yourself." His eyes traveled to Ilan who faced away, still observing Bonden.

Yanda had forgotten about her state of undress, her mind filled with healing her friend. "Thank you." She sent her drying skill over her body, then pulled on her suit.

Ilan touched her shoulder. "You should eat, too. You gave a lot just now."

Yanda could tell Mnenu fought a scowl. Would these men keep competing to take care of her? She felt drained. Scrambling over the edge of the pool, she gave Bonden's cheek a kiss. "I'll be back. You eat. Soon we'll have you out of the pool and you can do other things. I think they've set up a bed for you."

Bonden nodded a weak smile.

Yanda climbed down and said to Soni, "We'll bring you food. And give you a break."

"She should only need a short while in the pool." She glanced around at the plant life that covered trellises on the walls. "Seems like a healthy environment, probably more so than anywhere else on board. A bed near the pool is a good idea."

Merne entered, butt-pushing the door as she balanced a tray of soup and snacks. "It stays warm and moist in here, and there's less *grav* on this level. Would it be ideal to make a bed over there?" She cocked her head toward an alcove out of range of the lap pool, surrounded by vines and ambient lighting.

Chela pushed through the doorway with a basket of bread rolls under one arm, holding Zami's hand. Someone had dressed him in night clothes.

Yanda felt a pang of guilt that she hadn't noticed who was caring for her son.

"We can try her there," Soni said. "The Flari is near, so that's good. That's the main thing. The air moisture might be high."

"We can adjust that," Tlalit said over the comm system. "You have to anchor the bed."

Yanda chuckled. Tlalit could seem mellow but she'd wired to hear what's happening in every part of the ship and could enforce the controls staying on. Yanda'd heard her and Merne arguing about it.

She asked Soni, "Do you need to be back in Pedore?"

"I have a while," Soni said. "Maybe I could have a bed in here, too, to stay close." Something in her eyes made Yanda wonder if she really wanted to get back to Alland.

"Let's go below. You can eat. I'll check on Tlalit," Mnenu said to Yanda, glancing at Ilan. At her worried frown, he added, "You can always come back up."

"Closest bathroom?" Soni asked.

Merne set the tray down on a low table. "Right out the door. I'll bring bed pans though." And she left.

Yanda waited, still unsure. Soon Soni returned. Merne came with bedding. Chin and Jejods carried in bed frames.

Yanda hoisted Zami into her arms and nuzzled him. "Was it good, swimming like a fish?" she asked.

"Yeah. Did we make Bonden better?" His luminous swirling eyes raised to hers.

"I think we did. We tried hard, didn't we? And you helped. I could feel it."

"I wanted to swim with you in the color pool. Or the long one. Be salamanders."

"We will, Button. We'll do that together. Let's eat and then come back and check on Aunty Bonden before we sleep."

"Okay." He wriggled to the floor. He liked to go down the stairs on his own because gravity let him half-float, swooping.

Yanda followed, jumping down two at a time. He looked back over his shoulder and she crouched like a frog, bounding several steps and catching him. He laughed, making her chase him.

In the control room, Mnenu had taken over the ship's nav to let Tlalit help set up a medic area for Bonden. The Jejod sisters had returned to the control room to advise on navigating the skies of Erzon; it was their home world and they knew it best.

"What should we do?" Mnenu asked Aktat. "Go into the city or hover here? That uses up a lot of resources, I think. And we do need to restock."

Yanda sat in one of the strapping seats at the side, Zami resting his head on her shoulder.

Ilan came in and settled next to her, eating a vegan grilled cheese sandwich.

"Oh yes, thank you." Yanda grabbed half and broke off part, popping it in her mouth, giving Zami a piece.

"Nervy," Ilan said, swatting at her as if he minded. "Want your own?"

"It's okay. A bite's enough for now."

Jat said, "We think it might be best to take all of you to our family." She held a device, thumb hovering as if waiting for their decision.

"You have web access on that?" Ilan asked, peering at it.

"It's a bit tricky here but we have ways, yes." The middle Jejod sat, legs stretched out, and looked at her sisters.

"We want to show you our home," Tik said.

"But maybe more of what you need is in the city, especially for Bonden's recovery." Aktat looked pensive.

"What things? We can get them anything they need." Tik was clearly the most enthusiastic about sharing their home world with the visitors.

"But," Jat said, "the ground is different than you're used to."

"It's not always solid," Aktat added.

Chin ducked in, carrying a plate heaped with sati fries smothered in thick, savory sauce. She popped one in her mouth before taking a seat in the row.

They all stared out at clouds.

"Is it hard to navigate to your town?" Mnenu asked as Tlalit walked back in. He gave her his seat and Tik moved for Mnenu to sit next to her.

The Jejods chuckled, wheezy hisses.

"It's not exactly a town," Jat said.

"It's trees, mostly," Tik explained.

"Oh, like Rotoul," Mnenu suggested.

The bird-heads nodded slowly, thoughtfully.

"Sort of." Tik had her hand over her beaky mouth, still smiling. "You'll see. It just—"

"Could be strenuous," Aktat offered. She bit into a pear-shaped cabbage.

"There aren't exactly beds, either," Jat pointed out.

Yanda groaned. She liked a soft bed.

Tik noticed. "But we can make something you like," she promised perkily, then scowled at her sisters.

"Yes. We have the *sharran* floss," Jat cajoled Tik.

"Lots of it." Tik folded a leg nearly in two and embraced it, eyes excited.

"Okay, how do we do it?" Tlalit had a holo-screen up, checking nodes that glowed with numbers. "Come point out where I need to go. I will have to get into a city at some point for parts and supplies."

"It's not that far." Aktat came to stand by Tlalit. "How low are your supplies?"

"We can last a little while, if the ship rests, mostly shut down."

"I know a place." Aktat studied the vertical grid, then

pointed at the keypad. "You need to show coordinates in Erzon measures. May I?"

"Please." Tlalit pulled out an attached stool that swung from under the counter.

Aktat perched on it and tapped. Symbols popped up on the grid. Layers expanded until a 3D image appeared.

"Ooo." Yanda leaned forward, holding Zami who'd dropped off to sleep.

Ilan knelt close to study the topography.

Yanda realized Aktat must have adjusted the viewing windows of the ship. The solid clouds had transformed into a strangely colored atmosphere. Blues and greens shifted as if they moved through water. Ahead, they could now see land masses. Protruding cliffs gave way to a gash. They entered a deep ravine and then glided into a wide canyon, rising. Steep sides covered in ferns surrounded them. Tree trunks towered out of sight.

Aktat pointed. "It opens out there—a shelf you can land on."

A rock protrusion appeared ahead. As they skirted it, then lowered onto it with a rumbling hiss, they saw water-falls. A bird with a tall crest swept past their viewing windows. Others circled in the distance. Trees soared upward, strange fronds on the tops of the lowest.

The ship bumped and sank.

"Surface isn't right. I'm sinking through." Tlalit played madly with the instruments.

"There should be an anti-grav setting." Aktat leaned in and searched. "Here. Most ships these days are designed to set down on semi-solid worlds."

"This is a new one on me," Tlalit said, voice shakier than Yanda had heard it.

With barely a bump, the ship settle more securely.

"Okay. Shit. I thought we might sink clear in." Tlalit sat back with a throaty chuckle, chest heaving with deep breaths.

"What about walking out there?" Yanda asked.

"First, we'll run up to the house and get you some glasses," Jat said. "They have special lenses that will show you more accurately what you need to see. We got a load in for that party. Remember?"

"We think it's funny wearing them," Aktat explained.

"Didn't we get them for visitors?" Tik said.

Jat readied to leave the ship.

"I'm coming, too," Tik hurried after her.

"When did we ever have this many off-world visitors?" Aktat asked as her sisters left the control room, crossing the lounge toward the lower levels and exit.

"What's the atmosphere like?" Yanda asked Aktat. "Will we be able to breathe here?"

CHAPTER

9

Have you ever been in very high mountains?" Aktat asked. "It'll feel like that. Low oxygen."

"My home world is flat. Everywhere," Yanda responded, huffing a laugh.

"Move slowly, so you don't get dizzy," the Jejod advised.

"You haven't been home for years. Aren't you going with your sisters?" Yanda asked.

Aktat lowered her beak. "I had words with my parents before we left. I'm not sure what kind of welcome I'll get."

Yanda caught mind-speak from Jat and Tik to their sibling. "Come, Aktat!"

The eldest sister rose. With a gusty sigh, she strode away across the lounge after her sisters.

"I guess we wait." Yanda got up, lifting the sleeping Zami. "I'm going to check on Bonden. I'll put you here in the lounge, little guy." She gently laid him on the couch, covering him with a blanket and straightening, pressing her back.

"You should get a nap, too." Mnenu came up behind her and rubbed her shoulders.

"Mm, that's nice." She turned to him.

Vatu knelt by Zami. "I'll stay with him."

"I might take a quick swim," Mnenu said.

Ilan joined them. "I'd like to try that pool."

Mnenu looked suddenly stony.

"You should," Yanda said to Ilan, glancing between them. "It's wonderful." She led the way, the two men following.

Upstairs in the spa room, Yanda hurried to the corner where Bonden had been outfitted royally, a cascade of flowering vines behind her. Every movable comfort had been arranged around her; curtains blocked her bed from the pool. She sat propped against pillows, reading.

Yanda knelt by her. "You look so much better. How do you feel?"

Bonden's voice came slowly. "Strange. Better." She studied Yanda. "I'm so grateful. I want to know the whole story, how you got me out. What happened is fuzzy."

Ilan pulled up a camp chair on the other side and took Bonden's hand.

Mnenu jumped into the pool with a small splash.

"You were trying to get to me. I felt that," Bonden said to Ilan.

His forehead wrinkled with concern. "I was able to pull this very able crew to help me at last."

"You look like you're recovering from bruising," Bonden said, gruff, scrutinizing.

"Yeah, a couple times I tried entering disguised as a guard. They caught me. I think that's why they moved you."

"But you got away." Bonden's mouth quirked up.

He shrugged.

"How long were you in captivity?" Yanda asked her.

Bonden's face puckered as she thought.

"She was taken thirty-three turns ago." Ilan answered for her.

"What did they want with you?" Yanda asked.

"It's a bit early for grilling, isn't it?" Ilan gave Yanda a stern stare.

But Bonden squeezed her hand and said, "It's okay. Mostly they were experimenting with my powers, trying to get me to reveal them."

"You said, 'I won't do it,' like you were talking to them," Yanda said. She wished Ilan would swim as he'd planned and leave them to talk. She patted Bonden's hand. "Ilan's right. I'll let you rest. Do you mind people swimming in your bedroom?"

"Not at all. I'm happy to have company."

At poolside, Yanda stripped off her coverall, revealing an outfit of ocean blues made by the sea elves of Zotoul. It became a sort of second skin when she went *lanten*. Smooth as a porpoise, she took a gliding dive into the water and swam deep. When she came to the surface, Bonden was climbing into the pool naked.

Mnenu, Ilan and Yanda swam to her.

"Are you up to swimming?" Yanda asked.

Soni came from where she'd been doing something in her makeshift medical clinic in the corner. Yanda hadn't noticed her. She glanced at the bed, then examined who was in the lap pool. Approaching, she squatted at the edge. "Bonden, we can make the healing pool more tepid. You should really be in monitored waters."

"I feel fabulous," Bonden said, sinking into the refreshing temperature of the forty-foot saltwater pool.

Yanda scooted along the pool edge to Soni. "She's recovering quickly. She should probably do what feels good, in moderation, don't you think? These waters are most likely healing, with their ocean qualities."

Soni nodded, still hesitating.

"You could probably even go back to Alland," Yanda said.

"Do you think so?" Soni seemed unsure.

"You're so needed there in Pedore." Yanda was digging, curious why Soni had seemed to want to get away. "But I'm glad you're here. What would we have done?"

"I didn't do much. It turned out you all had what she needed."

"No, that's not true." Yanda looped an arm over the poolside. "We wouldn't have known how to set the Flari."

Soni shrugged. "I'm not sure that's what healed her. As for returning to Pedore..." Concern creased her brow as she glanced at the others.

Yanda climbed out of the pool. "Let's talk." She shifted to human, dried instantly, and dressed.

Down in the kitchen, the two sat at the table, hands folded around hot, lidded mugs. Gravity was erratic in the Erzon atmosphere. Sitting was a matter of hovering over seats.

In the next room, Zami squealed, playing with Vatu.

Yanda smiled, then sobered. "Tell me about what's happening in Pedore."

Soni took a sip of her *chaka* with healthy herbs added. "You know Jelat turned out to be a turncoat."

Yanda nodded.

"That discovery threw things into chaos. Cillen may

be in trouble with the government, and Arc has disappeared. No one's heard from him."

"For how long?" Yanda asked.

"Weeks." She made a worried grimace.

"They need you more than ever, then, don't they?" Yanda asked.

"Jelat's cronies have taken over."

Yanda thought of her apartment. She needed to ask Ilan to check on it.

"Families have left Pedore. It's not the place it used to be."

"Oh, no." Yanda gripped her cup. "This...is distressing." She'd appreciated the refuge next to the sacred crater, Satarn. "I feel guilty, that I left and never checked back. Just focused on my own problems."

"You have your daughter to find."

Yanda's eyes filled with tears. "True." She swallowed past a painful lump in her throat and pushed the thought down deep. They were doing all they could. Weren't they? "Will people set up another refuge?"

"They already are. I think a small center will be left in Balyou but any true refuge will be far out of town."

"That seems smart."

"With way better monitoring than last time." Soni sipped, face sad.

Ilan wandered in, drying his short red hair. He sat, hooking one leg under the chair to anchor himself. "I'm sorry about what's happening on Alland."

"I heard you helped finance the new location," Soni said.

Ilan shrugged. "I wish I could be there to help. Too many fires to put out."

They were starting to fix a meal when the Jejods

returned. Seeing the three in the kitchen, they entered, Jat carrying a sack. She set it on the table and opened it. The three sisters pulled out odd eyeglasses with dark indigo lenses.

"Everything okay at home?" Yanda asked.

"Yes. It's okay for all of us to go there." Being eldest, Aktat was often the spokesperson.

Soni's brow puckered. "Should we bring Bonden? She should maybe be near the Flari."

"Tlalit needs to shut things down to reserve energy stores," Jat said. "Besides, we have much healing ability. And it is better not to have too much weight on this promontory for long."

Eyes widened as the group took in this information.

Yanda asked. "What, we'd sink into… semi-solid… goo and suffocate?"

"We'd better get Bonden well, then, so she can go in for us if that happens," Ilan half-joked.

"The readings are fine," Tlalit said from the control room, listening in as usual. "Let's go up, see what it's like."

Aktat folded her arms, looking stern. "We can use a hover to collect supplies for you in Deladar."

"Or on Prokit's Moon," Tlalit said, hopefully.

The way he always talked about that moon made Yanda want to go there. What was so exciting about it? Apparently there was a lot of music and culture. She had to wonder, out of all the universe for this well-traveled, brilliant, peach-peak-haired Elf, what made it stand out.

"Deladar has everything you need. And we know suppliers. But if there's time, we can get you to Prok!" Aktat chuckled.

"Did the Sandu ships get away? What's happening

with the search? Do we know?" Yanda asked.

Merne said, in mind-speak from the control room, "They lost them, and so have we, but they're hovering outside the cloud area. I suspect they'll go to Prokit's Moon to wait for a new reading. They don't dare bring their ships in here. There's very little information available to nonlocals about setting the screens the way the Jejods did for us."

"Good hideout. Are there lots of bandits here?" Ilan asked.

Aktat drew up to her full imperious height. "Jejods have no trouble knowing who's in their cloud world."

"Oh, good." Ilan lifted a cup in salute.

The twelve lined up near the exit chambers, funny glasses in hand.

Bonden asked, "Shouma didn't stay?"

"She returned to her granddaughter," Merne said.

"You're not needed there on Sandu, Chela?" Yanda asked.

"I'm really not. They have plenty of healers and sophisticated medical staff. I think Shouma just wanted..." She shrugged.

"Wanted you around. Don't we all," Bonden said.

Chela colored slightly, ducking her head, fond eyes on Bonden.

Tlalit released the first exit door with a *pshh*. "We won't need oxygen masks?" she asked the Jejods.

"We could bring a couple in case," Aktat suggested. "Truth is, we haven't had a huge number of off-world guests here."

With each of the three airlocks, Yanda tested, checking Zami. "You okay?"

Zami nodded, holding his small elephant, carved by

Beri, Yanda's friend from earliest days of captivity, Zami's since soon after he was born though it was months before they met in person, only in their minds. Zami'd kept it on every world.

The final door slid aside and the ramp lowered. They gazed out at clouds, then put on the unique lenses. Land forms took shape. Towering trees clung to a glossy, dark hillside. Yanda wanted to touch it and see if it was sticky.

They filed out. The smell reminded Yanda of their hydroponics room, green but also a tad tangy. Soil and wind combined with that unfamiliar slightly acrid taint. They stepped onto the rubbery surface, feet sinking in. Suction grabbed at Yanda's boots, which was annoying.

Soon they were climbing among tree trunks. High above, Yanda saw rope structures. Able to see dizzying heights now, she let out a low moan and looked around at her companions, whose brows raised as well.

Mnenu pulled on a root to gain purchase, then held out a hand to her on a straight-up stretch. Gravity was much weaker than on Alland or Terlond, and she bounced up next to him with an easy pull.

"Get down?" Zami asked, squirming in Yanda's arms. She feared he'd slip into a hole or plummet downward on this strange surface, but set him by Mnenu who took his hand firmly.

Tik ran back and swept Zami to her shoulders. Laughing, she shot effortlessly up a tree. Yanda watched her bounding high above them, from tree to tree. Then she swept out of sight. It looked like she flew, though any wings were invisible.

"These are for the elderly," Jat showed them a rope lifts.

The fugitive fems had learned how to rise in Rotoul. They and the Elves ascended with Jat, while Aktat showed Soni to a woven basket on a pully. She came up slowly below them.

From an eyrie of broad proportions, Yanda lifted her glasses. Still only clouds. Yet she should be able to see through. She saw through alright, but only to more clouds. How did the glasses filter out cloud mass? Who had invented them? Were there science labs? Probably in Deladar.

They walked along tree limbs, and on mat bridges. Yanda detected signs of a city in the trees, of sorts. This world of the Jejods was different from the elven forest home, less advanced with creature comforts, more about perches for flight, nests fit between. Soon they arrived at a gathering of Jejods, where the clicking language filled the air. Non-humanoid birds flew about and perched close, part of the Jejod community. The tree tufts seemed made for treehouses, with flat broad limbs in places, other limbs protruding vertically to form levels for platforms and mazes of rooms. Zami squealed, climbing into branching rafters.

The first male Jejod Yanda had ever met chittered excitedly to Zami. Yanda edged closer. Zami tilted his head to listen, then tried out words he'd learned from Tik.

"*Takra tee tooda kroot,*" it sounded like to Yanda.

The elder male Jejod threw back his head and laughed, a cawing sound. Another elder—slightly bent at the shoulders, hair-feathers white and gray—brought Zami what looked like a sticky delectable pastry covered in seeds. Light shone through it. Where did the light come from? With the constant cloud cover, Yanda realized sun did penetrate. Adjusting to the glasses, she saw swirls of sunbeam roll in and out.

"Are there less dark versions of these glasses?" she asked Jat.

"You can adjust them," Jat said, reaching and sliding a finger along the rim.

Light cast in, striking every surface with more color and detail. Yanda saw symbols twining on posts, spiraling up limbs.

In the distance, down in a crevice of the hills, a sphere took shape, dark, semi-opaque. She turned to ask and noticed that many Jejods had gathered close to the three sisters, backs to her. They stood close, shoulders pressed together. Was it a meeting?

Yanda studied the sight. Then she looked around. "Bonden?"

"We have taken her to our healing place," Aktat said.

If there had ever been a rift between the Jejod sisters and their family, she felt no tension or conflict now.

"Would you like to see?" Aktat asked.

"I would," Yanda said.

They crossed more bridges of twine suspended over heart-stopping drops and came out into a fern valley of cascading pools. Yanda's eyes seemed to be adjusting to the colors, adapting to their quality. She lifted the glasses...and saw no clouds. Had her brain adjusted?

She stepped close to Vatu on a promontory above the valley. Bird chatter was constant. Breezes rushed up the hills and rattled tree fronds. The scents that wafted reminded Yanda of no tree she'd ever smelled, like dry grasses but more pungent. "Are your eyes adjusting? Try taking off the glasses."

"Oh, yes, I think so." Vatu slid the glasses into a shoulder bag.

Yanda asked others. Soni still saw clouds. Ilan seemed somewhere between, a slight mist remaining. Those who could, floated down into the valley, Tik leading the way to a pool where Bonden lay in a sphere of light on a warm stone.

Those of the group who wore clothes, stripped and jumped into pools.

"You never described the paradise here," Yanda said to Jat, simmering in a hot spring. Mnenu had taught her to remain non-*lanten* in water when she chose.

"We didn't talk about it a lot because we missed home terribly. And were worried." "Because" sounded like "becoss".

"I understand." Yanda knew all too well how it felt to come home to parents who disapproved, even if her leaving hadn't been her choice. "I saw a building, round, spherical, black, down in the hills."

Jat shook her head, ducked her beak into the water and flicked a spray out in an arc. "It's a research station." Her words seemed innocuous enough, but there was a hooded look about her nictating eyes. "I'd better check about where you'll stay." She rose out of the water, long limbs shoving up, and shook herself all over, sending spray in an arc. She leapt to the rocky lip of the pool, feet curling over the edge, and dropped, then swooped upward.

Mnenu scooted next to her, laughing. "That was abrupt. What'd you say to her?"

Vatu dove in.

"Where were you?" Yanda asked. "Where's Zami?" Panic sprang up in her.

CHAPTER

10

No worries. Tik has him. There's a kids' area."

"You followed him? You're a better mother than me!" Yanda sank to her nose, closed eyes burning with unshed tears.

Vatu put her rubbery fingers on Yanda's shoulder. "Don't be silly. You thought he was in good hands and he was."

Yanda pushed up to her chin in the water. "I didn't even make sure Bonden was being cared for. I was just curious and staring around."

"You can't always be the caretaker. You do more than your share. Right now, you deserve to rest and relax." Vatu took her hand and dove.

Yanda went along and they somersaulted. The three seemed to have the pool to themselves.

"I'm going to a colder one," Mnenu announced, shooting out of the water. He needed a steady diet of *lanten*, it seemed, for his color to look healthy. He jumped from pool to pool, enjoying the contrasting temperatures.

Their pool was at about the middle of the slope, so she could see above and below.

"I want to see the kiddy pool," Yanda said.

"There's a chute. Very smooth, like glass." Vatu sensed spaces like Yanda saw through them.

"Let's go."

Their eyes were wide with excitement as they scuttled across hillside to the entrance Vatu detected. Since first transforming to sea creature form, Yanda had found a new childlike place in her heart that could spring up, letting worries dissolve. Daring replaced caution. They giggled as they eyed the steep angle of the slide. Vatu jumped on, landing on her butt and skimming away. Yanda followed close behind. They screamed, whoops echoing. And shot out onto a pool of perfect tepid heat. They climbed to a shelf next to a flowing channel that gave them a view of another large pool below. Bird-people lifted miniature forms of themselves. Kids dove, then flew. In shallows, children and adults fluffed what seemed to be invisible wings.

"They really do have transparent wings, don't they?" Yanda pondered, chin on fist.

"I think they do, yeah. I wondered, when they soared to the tops of walls in the tunnel out of Dondar." Vatu languidly paddled.

"Should we check on Shouma? Find out where we're staying?" Yanda suggested.

"Look at you. You don't have to be on every second." Vatu gently flicked water drops at her.

"I suppose not. But I want to see if Tlalit stayed on the

ship. She should come enjoy this." Yanda sent mind-speak to their ship captain. "Are you still on the *Sarsefi*?"

"Can't you look through everything and see where I am?" Tlalit asked.

Yanda smiled, hearing the teasing in her mind. "That'd be a lot of work. Easier to ask you."

"What's it like out there?" Tlalit asked.

Yanda sent her mind-pictures, like a live streaming video, of the Jejod families in the large pool.

"Looks *sassafrastic*!" Tlalit said. She'd picked up strange words on her travels. "I got worried about the way the ship sank in when we first landed. Just wanted to make sure there was no damage in the lower areas."

"And was there?"

"No. It's fine. I found an extra pad that can be expanded. I lifted the ship, put out the floaters, and repositioned."

"Good on you," Yanda said, admiring the clever Elf-woman. "Can you come up here now?"

"Yeah, show me where. Merne will jump me there— so to speak." She gave a throaty chuckle.

Yanda sent an image of their location by the pools. In the next instant, the two handsome elves landed on the rock shelf with Yanda.

"Mmm, yes." Merne started undressing, eyes on the water.

"There's a hotter pool. Maybe you want to start there," Yanda suggested.

"Show us." Tlalit pulled off her ship suit.

Vatu joined them as they shot through the air and came down next to the pool where they'd started.

Yanda's clothes still lay on the strange, putty-like land

formation. "I'm going to see how Zami's doing." She picked up her clothes letting let the air hold her to drift down languidly to the side of the kids' pool. Vatu followed.

"Mama," Zami called into her mind.

She sought him, scanning the pool, and spotted him with Tik and others from their group in a cavern that glowed with coruscating colors.

"We're fishing," he said.

Vatu, sensing how to get there, led to a tunnel between pools and they emerged in time to see Zami leap to catch a rainbow fish. It wriggled in his hands, then he threw it in an arc into a stream that ran from the mouth of the cave.

Something else adjusted in Yanda's mind. As she attuned to this world's colors, she heard more sounds and caught thoughts being tossed about. She could almost see words hurtled and batted.

"Vatu," she said as they watched the fish-toss. "I heard my parents when we were in the pools on the ship. Did you hear them?"

Vatu said thoughtfully. "Yes, at least it seemed to be your parents."

"Do you think it was just my mind, a memory?"

"No, someone spoke to you. They urged you to use more of your powers. And you did."

"You think they're alive somewhere? I haven't dared to believe that. Always told myself they must be dead or they wouldn't have left me." Yanda's throat tightened with a familiar tug of abandonment and grief.

"They called you Yandawi, too."

"The elves and others know that name. It's probably from a myth." Yanda's monotone belied her deep emotion.

"Didn't Zamani say it's your true name?"

"Whatever that means. He said it. Tenali said it. I think the guy in Pedore—Arc—even used it."

"What are you going to do?" Vatu asked.

Yanda noticed Zami's gaze on her, and waved, clapping to cheer him on. "You mean try to reach them? Figure out where they are?" Yanda asked, breathing hard with the frustration of never having known anything about her parents. "I think I'll ask Ilan to help me find out."

Vatu squeezed Yanda's arm. "That's a good idea. A very good idea."

"It is?" There was something in Vatu's manner that raised Yanda's curiosity.

"I noticed...when we heard those voices talking to you, Ilan's eyes opened wide. He grew very still, very intent. Like maybe he was trying to..."

"Trace them?" Yanda suggested, her heart hammering.

"Yeah, like that," Vatu said.

Yanda heaved a sigh—of relief to have shared that with Vatu, received some confirmation?—before they pushed off and swam to Zami.

Dinner took place in a semi-round perch high in the trees. They ate stacks of crunchy sticks and straws, a mushy mound Yanda thought was mushroom, tender moist wafers with a delicate scent like lotus, bamboo shoots in sauces. "This is all so lovely," she said, resisting the urge to ask about every single thing.

"I'm going to go back to the ship for the night," Tlalit announced.

"We can have it watched, but it's up to you," Aktat said. "I should have realized there would be landing discs."

"No harm done. When do you think we might get supplies? I've made a list." Tlalit brought up a screen in front of her. It adjusted to face whoever was looking at it. "Add to it if you have needs."

Other items appeared on the list.

"Alright. Not too much." Tlalit grinned. "Bonga beans? Really? Who added that?" She looked around.

There were snickers. Hardly anyone liked bonga beans.

Their hosts prepared rooms with woven siding. Jejods tended to sleep on limbs as they could perch anywhere without fear of falling.

"I hope we're not putting your people out too much," Yanda commented to Jat, the cordial and reserved middle sister.

"They are highly pleased by your presence," the Jejod said.

The visitors gathered on a platform under stars. At least Yanda saw stars. She wasn't sure how many of their group had adjusted to seeing past or through clouds. "I wonder how Shouma and her son got away," she said in a low voice to Aktat.

"They have very tricky ways of disguising. They spent a little time in Deladar and remade their ship's identity inside and out. Then left Erzon in a different direction than they came."

Merne made an elven fire at the center. For the visitors, it provided heat and brightness. The Jejods, who saw well at night, didn't seem to build any type of fire.

"The Qontaqian ships will not come into the clouds," Aktat said, confident. "And if they do..." Her expression hinted at dire consequences.

"That's reassuring," Yanda said.

Aktat made a bow and turned to the male Yanda thought was her father.

Yanda moved over to Ilan. "Can we talk?"

The burly Qontaqian brought his gaze to her, surprised out of deep brooding. "Of course." He immediately stood from a woven bench that ran along the side of the platform.

Yanda caught Vatu's eye. Zami lay asleep on the Mingali's lap, feet stretched onto Chela, who rested a fond hand on his leg. The women assured her in mind-speak that they would take care of him.

As she and Ilan stepped onto a bridge that ran far between trees, she noticed Mnenu watching. She gave him what a reassuring smile, then walked toward a crossroad of woven spanners, trying not to look down. Behind her, wood and woven reeds creaked with Ilan's weight. A few times, she caught him glancing over the hand rail to the drop far below but kept her own eyes up.

"Can we take this one?" He pointed to a connecting ramp to a pointed mountain peak. "I like solid ground."

"As solid as it gets here," Yanda said, grinning. "Sure." She started off, nimbly traversing the distance, slowing at the middle where it dipped lower, then hurried to the end, where a rock shelf jutted, and swung onto it. The rock was pliant, with that putty feel. She sat in a natural seat formed in the wall of an arched alcove. From there, she gazed out over treetops at stars and a lavender crescent moon.

"Do you still see clouds?" she asked as Ilan settled next to her.

"It's like I'm seeing both, the clouds and what's inside them."

"Wow. Everyone must see something different here," she said.

"Something on your mind?" he asked, shifting his back to sit more comfortably.

She turned to him. "When we were in the pools on the ship, when Bonden—"

"Your parents?" he asked.

"Vatu thought you might have—" She hunched toward him, eager— "maybe been able to trace where they are?" Her voice had dropped low and soft, like she was ready to bite back the words.

"I did try," he said, taking her hand. He scooted closer and brushed hair from her eyes. "I think we can." He leaned in and studied her face.

She sat up straighter and stared down the ramp they'd crossed. A figure was there, black against black.

CHAPTER

11

Yanda searched for a mind-print. All she needed was the briefest thought. And she caught it. It was Mnenu. He must have followed them.

At the touch of her mind, he turned away. She thought about calling after him, but she and Ilan were talking. That was all.

He could have made himself invisible but he didn't. She watched him returning to the place where the hanging paths met, and move on. She remained silent.

"Was that Mnenu?" Ilan asked.

She nodded.

"I don't want to cause trouble between you two."

"Yes, you do." She laughed. "Don't you?" She stood to go.

He put a hand on her waist, hot through her bodysuit. Tingles ran through her. Guilt, also.

She'd been thinking this trip wasn't doing the sea elf

any good. His color wasn't what it had been on Terlond, despite swimming in the Terlondian waters of the lap pool.

Nevertheless, it wouldn't be right to let herself...

Ilan's strong hand tugged her closer, just a fraction. She could sit on his lap, rest her head on his shoulder, be held. She wanted to melt into that.

Instead, she pulled away and ran along the rope bridge, breathing hard. She didn't even check back to see if he followed. She kept going until she reached the meeting room. The group remained talking. Glad she hadn't stayed away longer, she searched for Zami.

"I'll show you where you're sleeping." Jat pulled her to a rope ladder.

Floating lights hovered above them as they made their way along tree-roads, through frond-halls and across woven landings until they stepped into a cozy basket-shaped room. Zami slept soundly under puffy blankets. Vatu sat reading in a similar nest, an empty bed humped up between them.

"Tlalit sent up your backpack." Jat pointed.

In the night, Yanda drifted from a dream of tumbling off the platform, falling, falling... She felt Ilan's mind on alert, then Bonden's.

"There's a darkness," Bonden moaned, "in my soul."

Yanda gave Jat a mind-call. "Are you sleeping?"

"We Jejots sleep lightly. I'll take you to her."

Yanda whispered to Vatu, "Stay with Zami?"

"Call if you need me," Vatu said, wide eyed with worry. She pulled Zami into her bed.

As Jat and Yanda dropped from the last ladder, Ilan met them with Aktat. They ran for the entrance to the clinic where Bonden was sequestered. A Jejod Yanda didn't remember meeting sat attentively next to Bonden's bed.

Bonden reached out a hand to Yanda.

Yanda pulled a stool close and sat, taking it. "I think we should get everyone," she said to the others.

Ilan said to the attending Jejod nurse, "I think we'll be filling the space around the bed. There will be healers so feel free to take a break, or the rest of the night." He gave her an ingratiating smile.

The Jejod nurse stood and waited to see who would take her place.

"Don't disturb anyone's sleep on my account," Bonden said, forehead crinkling.

"Too late." Yanda kissed the woman's cheek. It felt too cold.

Mnenu walked in. He took in Yanda and Ilan already next to the bed and frowned. Behind him filed in others: Tik, Vatu carrying Zami, Chela, Soni, and Chin. Chela moved to the bedside and nodded to the Jejod nurse. "We can care for her. Thank you."

Merne and Tlalit called that they'd help from the ship.

Shouma joined in the mind-meld from Sandu. "Let's go in and see what this darkness is. It's a good time to do follow up on the clearing we started two days ago."

"I'd be grateful."

By now, ten squeezed around the bed.

Bonden scooted up higher, seeming self-conscious of all the attention. When Tlalit and Merne entered, the circle around the bed made room and all held hands.

"Don't we want to get her into the Flari?" Yanda asked.

"Yanda, I think it would help if you first do a diagnostic, taking Chela and Soni in with you, through Bonden's physical body. Once that's done, let's see what we have."

"Good idea." Soni was standing by screens where tubes connected to Bonden. "I see a few worrisome numbers."

Yanda sent her sight into Bonden, starting in her brain and descending to her heart and other organs. Soni and Chela stayed with Yanda's mind. Yanda was a surgeon; she would see a lot but might miss healing aspects.

The three withdrew. Bonden stared, waiting for a prognosis.

"It's in the stomach-liver area," Soni said.

Chela and Yanda nodded agreement.

Soni's mouth set in a grim line. "You're right, Yanda. We should get her back into the Flari."

Shouma said, "There's something the healing waters alone cannot solve related to her powers. But the Flari is important as well, to help her stabilize. Merne can bring her by instant travel."

"I wonder if that's a good idea," the Elf woman, daughter of the leader, countered. "Going between takes her into the between, where others have access. Even though it's just an instant. Maybe she should be carried."

"We can float her without jostling," Aktat said.

"Tlalit, can the ship take all our weight?" Yanda asked.

"It can now, yes, with the floats extending under," Tlalit said.

Shouma said, "It should be as before. Yanda in the tub with Bonden, Soni monitoring. Vatu and Mnenu in the pool."

"And Zami. He was in the pool, too." Yanda gathered

him from Vatu's lap and kissed his cheek. "Want a nighttime swim?"

He nodded, fully awake now, though fatigue pulled at his eyes.

"He can lie on Bonden's bed if he gets tired." Yanda started toward the downward slope.

"Chela and Ilan should be close by," Shouma went on. "The rest can gather together by mind, holding the healing meld, helping to detect what is hidden."

Ilan followed closely after Yanda, drawing a glance and frown from Mnenu, who hurried to catch up. Yanda caught fleeting thoughts from Mnenu. He had a role too, in the pool. But Ilan? He just tinkered with his AI. Yet he got to be right there, involved with all the intricacies with Yanda.

She sent Mnenu a gentling mind-message. "I value your presence."

His head turned toward her and he gave her a self-deprecating smile. "And I yours."

The Jejods carried Bonden down between them in a hammock, sweeping through the air. Once the woman was safely lowered to the ship, Chin carried her easily up through low-grav levels to the regeneration pool.

Yanda felt wetness on her neck as Zami slept, head on her shoulder. She'd used the strap-on carrier to navigate the steep slope, floating at times.

Entering the ship, she tested the solidity with a few jumps, jostling Zami but not waking him. Others followed behind her in a long line to the warm, moist spa room with its fecund smell of living foliage. Low lights revealed Soni, already concentrating on settings. She poured liquid amendments into compartments on her side.

Chin and Chela undressed Bonden and eased her into the waters.

Mnenu and Vatu dove into the long narrow pool.

Vatu held out blue arms to Yanda. "Give me Zami?"

Yanda stroked the boy's cheek with a thumb. His face was less pillowy every day, losing his baby fat, but still smooth as velvet. "Darling, want to swim?" she said softly, close to his leaf-shaped ear.

He opened tired eyes and smiled, nodding. Groggily, he climbed out of Yanda's arms and toddled unsteadily to Vatu.

"Let's get you nakie!" Vatu pulled him into her arms and he helped get off his nightsuit. Vatu lifted him and the two jumped into the water together.

Yanda longed to be in the lap pool with her son and the others, but she had a different task.

Ilan stood at the end of the Flari like a sentinel. Yanda stepped around him to the stairs and tugged off her nightgown.

When she was submerged, Ilan rested a hand on Yanda's shoulder as she went *lanten*, and sank underwater with Bonden. He felt something of the shift, staying connected on a deep level. A tremor quivered in his belly as he realized he might grow to understand the transformation.

Ilan knew Yanda wanted his best effort at finding a trail to her parents. And through them, maybe her daughter. Perhaps he could find out if her sense that they were all on a moon in Unknown Space was accurate; he knew Yanda's vision had been tenuous.

Her skin, in sea creature form under his hand, turned slightly rubbery. She looked mostly the same, but for gills opening and closing at her waist. Her eyes were closed but he'd seen the *otherness* of them in *lanten* before: more animal, feral even, yet brilliant, fully conscious, powerful, scary, exciting.

Saving Bonden was paramount, and he would let nothing cloud his instincts. Taking up this station next to the Flari, with the two women inside, battling for Bonden's health and powers, he experienced an intense sense of responsibility. Fully in the mind-meld, he thrilled to delve into Bonden, down through her tissues and cells, seeing with Shouma, Yanda, Chela, and Soni's expert eyes, understanding what they saw through their minds. As the hive-mind swarmed toward her vital organs, the healing team detected toxicity. Something had been injected that remained in her, trying to read her powers, he had to assume—as well as to detect her location and keep track of her. They had invested in her; they would not let her go lightly.

The Jejods and Tlalit had explained that those from Qontaq hunting her could not penetrate the gases' refracting signals. Readings jammed in Erzon's atmosphere. But who knew what else they might have put in her, so far undetectable.

"Liver, spleen, stomach...it's in there," Soni said. "I can provide a specific cleansing blend. It will take me only a moment. But I suspect there's something nonmedical—"

"Powers. Magic," Ilan mumbled. He sent his mind into the AI that mirrored and communicated in his cerebrum as well as in the dark, hidden networks he used and found precedence for this type of incident. In a low murmur, he dictated several substances to Soni to check for correspondence.

Soni responded, "Those are ones I'm getting in my database as well." She had brought an advanced computer and set up a mini-lab on a side counter, with beakers and measuring devices from the greenhouse.

Ilan read off the percents.

"Two percent *icelent*? I thought maybe four." Soni pursed her lips.

Soni and Ilan went back and forth until Soni came over with pale yellow liquid in a syringe.

Yanda saw a stream of medicant enter Bonden's abdominal area.

Shouma and Chela took the substance and delicately distributed it to the affected organs.

Bonden detected what they were doing and tried to help, but Shouma gently told her, "Save your strength, my love. Just tell us any discomfort we might not detect."

Yanda, still breathing into Bonden's mouth, took in the formula of the substance from Ilan's mind, and with it, a stream of AI that coursed through her mind, creating an intelligence she could apply to the region. She had moved obstructions but had not cleansed an organ. Soni was in their minds as they spread the solution through each organ. It seemed to attach to the toxic material.

Though in synch with a dozen other minds, Yanda felt herself and Ilan growing a close bond in tandem with the AI. The toxicity needed to become effluent, drawn out, contained outside Bonden, and disposed of.

Suddenly Bonden lurched up out of the water. Shouma and Yanda made an opening above her navel and Soni was ready with a tube and flask. What oozed out had no real substance. Dark like smoke yet thicker, it threatened to reenter but Shouma stopped it, pulled, and when the flow tapered off, Soni stoppered it.

Merne appeared suddenly in the room, grasped the container and disappeared.

Yanda wondered briefly where she went. Hand to Bonden's belly, she sealed the tissues, mending cells.

Bonden sat back down in the water, tears streaming, and threw her arms around Yanda. They rocked and cried, Bonden for the shock of it, Yanda right there with her in all the emotions.

After a time, Soni suggested Bonden stay in the bed on the ship so she could be monitored. Bonden agreed, too exhausted to argue, glad to not be alone. Hands helped her from the pool and into bed.

Tired but relieved, most of the *Sarsefi's* passengers climbed or soared back up toward their accommodations with the Jejod. Vatu rose with Zami.

Ilan and Yanda followed at a short distance. Near a shelf jutting into shadow, Ilan took Yanda's arm. "I want to tell you something."

She lifted a brow but followed, exhausted. She stumbled as they crossed from the stone protrusion onto soil. She tripped on roots and stones. A natural bench had been carved facing a vista out over a valley. A glimmer of sunrise touched the horizon. Ilan pulled Yanda next to him on the seat.

"What?" she asked, almost chuckling at how they played out the same scene from the night before. They seemed to be forever sitting down together, nearly becoming intimate, then chasing off after another emergency.

He wrapped an arm around her and she let her head drop onto his shoulder. Before she could fall asleep, he pulled away and lifted her face to him so their eyes met.

Her lids drooped but when she saw his intense gaze, she straightened. "Were my parents there?" Adrenalin pumped through her, raising her pulse.

"They were. They didn't want to interrupt the work you did. But they felt that toxic material keenly. It drew them urgently. They know something about it."

"Did you catch where they are?"

He shook his head. "They'll be in touch, Yanda."

"Oh, moons. That's..." She shivered. From cold? From the news of her parents? She was too tired to sort it out.

He pulled her onto his lap, assuming she shook from cold.

She pulled her head back to look at him. He was comfort. They'd worked so closely.

He bent to her lips.

She said, "Mm..." briefly stirred by the contact. Then dropped to sleep on his shoulder.

CHAPTER

12

Yanda woke to find Zami snuggled into her bed. Unfamiliar sounds and smells were in the air: high whistles and clicks, drips and whistling through the strangely colored, bottle brush tree fronds. The scent of greenery was wet with the cloud bank that always surrounded it; the fact that she could see through the clouds didn't mean they weren't there. Rifling in her backpack, she found knit hats for her and Zami, to keep out the clamminess that felt damp in her ears and on her neck. As she pulled on her son's cap, he edged in closer. She squeezed him in a hug, smelling his familiar hair scent, sweet and musky. He breathed deep, content.

She remembered, then, the kiss. Ilan must have carried her here. Now that she'd rested, she recalled his lips on hers. She savored the memory, breathing slowly, smiling, imagining making love to him, wondering what it would be like after so much potent energy had passed between them. Their connection always had an undeniable volatile charge. But would that be good? What about Mnenu?

Suddenly she knew Ilan was awake and catching something of her thoughts. Her first instinct was to close him out. Why? She was embarrassed to be caught thinking of him, of *making love to him.*

"Can't sleep?" he asked into her mind.

She peered out through a narrow opening in the woven wall, gazing at pink light at the edge of a starry night sky. "I just woke," she said, wondering what it would be like to sleep with him, have his warmth against her, to wake in the night and talk. She felt sure she'd like that. "I think I'm sleepy enough to drift off again. You're having trouble sleeping?" She wanted his presence, and she didn't. So much trouble. They would probably...what? Argue? Fight?

"I haven't slept yet. Not your problem. You sleep."

"You were telling me my parents will contact me. How do you know?" Now that she remembered, she felt more awake.

"I haven't told you everything. But I want to talk about it when we're together."

Hasn't told me everything? Her mind raced then. What had he found out? Was there something he'd always known?

She didn't know why her mind went to suspicion. Well, all the tech rebels on Alland had known things about her and never seemed to share all with her. Arc, Jelat, and now Ilan. Others who were squatting in her apartment, the rebel camps in the outback. "Okay. Tomorrow?" She did long to burrow back into her pillow—a funny poofy affair provided by the Jejods—and fall into dreams.

"Yes. Good night, beautiful," he said.

Beautiful. That was the first term of endearment he'd used with her. At first, the absence of him from her mind left her cold and sad. She wiggled closer to her son, arm loose over him. It had been a disturbing day, discovering Bonden had the gunk of those evil Qontaqians in her. They had performed an extraction like nothing she'd experienced. Merne had taken it away. Where? Out into space? Destroyed it, hopefully. But maybe they wanted to study it. Had Merne sealed it safely?

Daylight arrived with bustle. Down on the ship, Tlalit prepared to go to Deladar for supplies. "Yanda, I need you," she called in mind-speak. "Will you come with us?"

"Bring the baby?" Yanda asked.

"Not this time."

"Ilan?"

"He's coming. He's already at the shuttle."

Yanda dressed, kissed Zami, hugged Vatu, and scurried down the hill, hurt that Ilan hadn't brought her with him.

"Where are you?" Tik hurried up to her, excited for the trip, and showed her the way.

The shuttle, a land vehicle that could float in air or on water, perched on a flat land mass. It had personality. The shape of a gumdrop, it could sprout long Jejod-like legs for difficult terrain, "where floating wasn't possible or advisable," Tik explained.

"This is the Koddler," Aktat said as they arrived. She gestured for Yanda to climb in the open passenger door.

Yanda pulled up the few steps, stuck her head into the

tall domed interior, and peered around before settling into the closest seat, next to Ilan who was already strapped in. Behind them were two more rows of three seats each. A cargo bay formed the rear. Tlalit swung in upfront, next to Aktat in the driver position. Yanda was by far the shortest at sixty-seven centimeters.

"Will the hold be big enough for what you need?" Aktat asked Tlalit. "We can bring a second Koddler."

"There's plenty of room. I mostly need parts and micro supplies. Nothing that large. The fuel is okay 'til we move on. Probably fill up on Prokit's Moon."

Aktat turned a beaky smile to Tlalit and chuckled. "You and your Prok obsession."

Tlalit turned her orange-peaked head away to peer out the window. She must suit the bird-like Jejods very well with her cockatiel style, Yanda thought.

Ilan turned to Yanda and sent her a private mind-message. "There's a library on Prok we should visit."

"Really?" Yanda looked at him. "You've been?"

"How long will we spend on Prok?" Ilan asked Tlalit.

"Oh, at least a week." She craned around to face Yanda. "If that's okay with you."

Yanda nodded, hands pressed together between her thighs. "We don't have absolute news of Seiti so... Anyway, I've heard so much about Prokit's Moon from you." She grew somber. "We may as well be there as anywhere."

Ilan had been tapping the keys of a device but his fingers stilled. Again, in private mind-speak, he said, "That's not entirely true. We do know a bit more."

Yanda made a face. More withholding?

He chose not to address it. "Prok's a good start, actually." He gave her an appeasing eye-crinkle.

Tlalit and Aktat conversed in the front as the vehicle lifted off and soared down into the valley. Yanda thought it was the one she'd faced from her bed-basket.

Tlalit used many Jejod terms, clicking and whistling well.

Soon Deladar came into view. It was the most unusual city Yanda had seen yet. Half aeries and birdcages, the streets had multiple levels, like an elaborate climbing structure, so that one looked through open spaces. Winged vehicles and large birds traveled throughout the airy layers, some carrying passengers or cargo.

As they descended, Yanda saw flowering vines twining along beams and poles. Music spilled from establishments glowing with float-globes and strings of colored lights.

Aktat slipped into a tall structure where other Koddlers and an array of unfamiliar vehicles were arranged on shelves. "We'll leave the Kod here and bring supplies or have them delivered." Each shelf had a symbol. Yanda made a mental note. Like Mnenu had taught her, she put it in a drawer where she could retrieve it. She had a feeling AI would help her sort a lot more information that way.

A clear cylindrical lift descended to the base of the parking structure. Yanda and Ilan took the chute while Tlalit and Aktat floated down. Yanda could have drifted on the air as well but chose to accompany the big man who wasn't quite as adept.

"What about Merne and Mnenu?" Yanda asked, guiltily realizing she hadn't thought about them before this.

"I left them," Tlalit answered. "They know the ship best and can watch over things while I'm gone."

"Didn't Tik want to come?" Yanda asked, suddenly remembering the younger sister had led her there and she'd never looked back.

"Tik can come here anytime. She has a special job today." Aktat had said all she was going to about that. She walked away.

As they stepped out onto a sidewalk, Ilan and Yanda stared up through the layers of the town.

"I'm glad things are tall here," Ilan said. "Whether they'll bear my weight is another question."

"They will," Aktat said, confident, though her limbs were bird-like and had to weigh next to nothing.

"I'll pick and choose where I enter. I mainly need a *steropel* and a few other obscure tech parts. No worries if I can't find them." Ilan indicated size with his fingers.

"That's right up the block. On ground level." Aktat gave a beaky smile. "Plenty strong for you."

"Fabulous." Ilan bowed his head. "Can you point the way?"

"I need a few things there, too," Tlalit said.

"We'll stop there first then." Aktat led them along the narrow sidewalk as vehicles passed, some like wheels for pet rodents, others like swizzers for individuals, most floating.

Yanda reminded herself that a stranger would see Deladar all in clouds, like a thick fog. The street angled upward.

After a few blocks, Aktat stopped in front of an intriguing storefront: boxes, wires, tiny domes, and light-filled bobbles protruded from strips of plaz on the building's face. The four filed in. Shelves were filled with items related to IT. Jejod clerks and customers floated up to the higher parts of the store to retrieve hard-to-reach items.

Yanda realized it wasn't just the hair; Tlalit had worn an outfit not unlike the Jejod sisters: dark martial jacket and pants, sides wrapping and tying. Her rubbery boots that gripped trees in Rotoul, with separate toes, resembled Jejod boots. She blended well. Yanda and Ilan did not fit in so easily. Was that a concern? Should Vatu have come along and disguised them? She sent a mental message to Zami. "Having fun?"

"I play with Auntie Vatu," he responded, calmly. "When you come back?"

"We won't be long. You have fun. Maybe go to the water with the other kids." She included Vatu on this part.

"We will," Vatu assured her. "There's also a large climbing structure I was told of. I thought I might take Zami there. Invite a few others his age."

"Thank you for doing this. Do you mind?" Yanda asked her.

"I'm having the time of my life. It's amazing here." Vatu sounded like she meant it. "Show us Deladar."

Yanda walked to the doorway. From a short distance up the hill, she turned to give a panorama of mental pictures.

"Wow." Vatu gazed with wonder. "Look where Mommy is."

Zami squealed, his hands clutching together with enjoyment at the sight.

The others came out.

"On to ship parts," Tlalit said.

"That'll be near the flight-port," Aktot explained.

"Is there something Yanda and I might do while you two cover that?" Ilan asked. "Have any suggestions?"

"My favorite is Ender's Café," Aktat said. "You can see

the whole town and parts of the lake from there, and they serve yummy fruit *whirs*." She explained the way there.

"You don't think the Qontaqs could have spies here, to you?" Yanda asked.

"Absolutely not," Aktat assured her.

Yanda wondered how they could get to Prokit's Moon safely, leaving the cloud space, but didn't push it for the moment. They climbed higher until they reached the tiki hut that was Ender's Café, and chose a table on the terrace. Sure enough, the view was dazzling. A lake below sparkled, large as a small sea. At this time of day, Prokit's Moon was visible, etched pale pink above the horizon.

A Jejod waiter, who looked like a teen, not that different from Tik but with more tats, sauntered over with tall drinks, straws made from thin reeds protruding at the tops.

When she'd gazed out enough, sucking on her berry *whir*, Yanda eyed Ilan sideways. "Ideal time for you to tell me what you know."

"Yes, it is," Ilan agreed. "I've wanted to get you alone. Really alone."

"Thanks for putting me to bed last night, by the way."

"No problem. I just carried you there. Vatu took care of the rest." His lips pressed in a hint of a shy smile.

Yanda raised her brows, considering a teasing remark but then said, "I want to know everything you've found out or sensed about my parents. However, first I'd like to hear…"

Ilan's brows shot up in surprise. "What would that be?" Shadow haunted his eyes.

What did he fear she'd ask? Yanda wondered. "If Jelat is a sell-out, what about Arc? I don't think Cillen is, from what Soni said."

Arc was an enigmatic figure, the first she'd met at Pedore, the refuge on her home planet. She'd loved the energy of his mind-speak. It was gentle, smooth as a soft-flowing stream. Yet he appeared to be teamed up with Jelat, seemed to have trusted him, put her in his hands. How could he not know Jelat was intending to betray her? That he was tied with the Sinisay, the planet's secret police that captured and exploited talents like hers, and Ilan's. All her allies.

"Arc is good as far as I can tell. He loves the crater called Satarn most of all. He almost seems made of the same soil. That's his sacred place. And being of skilled lineage, he wants to protect others who have powers."

"So he didn't guess what Jelat was up to?" She couldn't know if Ilan was being straight with her. Why was he so reluctant with the truth? If she couldn't trust him, should she even have him on this mission to find her daughter? Another question came to her: Just because Arc's mind communication seemed refined and gentle, could it be he was in fact naïve? Less powerful at reading others? "Why is it I don't always feel you're revealing all you know to me?"

He took her hand. His was warm, as always. For a moment, he studied the distance, not looking at her. Then brought his gaze back. "I know sometimes I feed you piece-meal."

"That's it." She pulled her hand away. "It'll turn out later that you already knew something important." Her heart raced and belly churned. She took a small sip of her melon-berry *whir* and breathed slow to settle her anger, suspicion, feeling of betrayal.

He spoke soft and slow. "I don't ever try to hurt you."

"I know you don't, but you do hurt me when you don't tell me what you know, things pertinent to me. To protect me?" Her voice went up in frustration.

"And Zami, yes."

"Or you don't trust that I can hide it?"

A frown creased his brow. "Maybe that's part of it."

She stomped her foot under the table, glancing at those around them, and hissed, "Then teach me," her teeth clenched. "If you think I'm that weak, teach me." Tears pricked her eyes.

His gaze traveled over her face. He squinted out to the far hills surrounding the cobalt lake, then looked back to her. "Teach you. Yes. Of course, I can teach you. I have to think about it. Can you give me a little time?"

"Well, of course I can." Yanda responded, throat tight. "What do you mean by a little time, though?"

Ilan took a long breath. His red *whir*, full of *kari berries*, native to Erzon, sat untouched. "I think, on Prok, we should get our own place, for several days." He took her hand again. "I don't know what kind of lessons Shouma did with you, but I imagine it might have been soft." His thumb stroked the back of her hand. "What I'd need to do...what *we'd* need is more bootcamp."

Yanda scrunched her eyes. "Yikes. Do we need a cabin on some desolate mountain side so no one will hear me screaming?" she deadpanned, afraid the answer might be yes.

"Uh. No, not screaming. But maybe a little miserable. If you're to fight off people like Bonden's attackers."

"Eh. Here I thought I was gonna have fun on Prok."

"You're the one who asked—"

"—to be taught. I know." She squeezed his hand, then

pulled away as Tlalit and Aktat appeared entering the veranda.

"What about Mnenu?" he asked.

"He doesn't seem well," Yanda said. "I think he should return to Terlond. To his seas."

Tlalit and Aktat spotted them and wove around tables toward them.

"Is that supposed to answer my question?" He smiled, showing teeth but not joy.

"I think so." She leveled her gaze at him.

"What are you two plotting over here?" Tlalit had a full bag over one shoulder.

"You lugged everything up here?" Ilan asked, standing and reaching out his hands.

"Oh, *dravis*, no. This is just a few gifts I picked up on the way from the garage." Tlalit took a seat, long legs angling past the table. Aktat did the same.

A waiter brought *whirs* and a platter of munchables they must have ordered on their way in. The waiter placed plates in front of each of them.

"Great." Yanda reached for a mounded cracker and jammed it in her mouth with a muffled *thank you*.

"Have we been starving you?" Tlalit asked with a deep chuckle as she scooped a lacy fritter into sauce. "Soni thinks Bonden should have a complete cleanse in a spa on Prokit. They have jeloli flushes there. Jeloli's a native flower with great cleansing properties. We should go soon." Tlalit bit the translucent food neatly.

"I'm ready," Yanda said.

"So am I." Ilan glanced at Yanda and nodded.

"Let's tell the others we'll go on tomorrow." Tlalit ate fast, as though anxious to get moving. "It'll be less stress on your family," she added to Aktat. "They've welcomed us so grandly."

Soon the platter of delicacies was gone and the group trundled downhill to the Koddler.

CHAPTER

13

That evening the Jejods provided a feast for the visitors. Musicians emitted flute sounds and those of creaking branches in a strong wind, similar to stringed instruments. Singers called disharmonic birdsong. Acrobats performed daring feats in the sky. Yanda thought she'd have to get used to the sounds, but the synchronized falling through the air took her breath away, sweeping back up in sheer elegance.

The plan was to sleep on the ship and get off first thing. They thanked their hosts and said goodbye, not knowing when or if they'd return to this amazing world.

The trip to Prokit's Moon would take little time with hyperdrive, Tlalit assured them.

"We have enough fuel for that. Then we need to fill up." Tlalit fidgeted, clearly anxious to go. They gathered belongings they'd brought to the treetop villa and paraded down the mountainside late in the night.

Back on ship, Yanda slipped away to her compact quarters with Zami for alone time. They lay on the bed and Zami told her about his day.

"Tomorrow we're going to Prokit's Moon. Tlalit has been talking about it since I've known her."

"What we do there?" Zami asked.

Yanda hugged him to her. "I think there'll be things you'll like. I don't know much about it."

"Animals?"

"Oh, I imagine so. Let's ask in the morning." She could look it up, read about it, but sometimes travel should be about discovery.

Vatu came and climbed in above them.

Drifting to sleep after a long day, Yanda thought, "We got the darkness out of Bonden." She wanted to congratulate herself and the others but something held her back. Was Bonden really safe now? Had they removed everything that threatened her? Soni's readings and their examinations told her she was free of taint. Yet worry niggled in her.

At dawn, the passengers and crew of the *Sarsefi* went through preparation for take-off with the ease of practice. Tik showed up. Jat and Aktat weren't coming. "I'll get a lift back here from Prok," she said. "Don't worry," when Tlalit's brow creased.

So none of the Jejods were going on with them. Yanda's heart fell. She'd loved having the fems, or most of them, together again, definitely stronger with all their talents. "What about Chin?" she asked. Chin had been attached at the hip to the Jejods.

"Maybe she and Bonden can get rides where they want to go from Prok," Tik suggested. "Travelers are always coming and going in every direction."

They strapped in. Tlalit started to ease off the shelf. The ship stayed where it was. Tlalit called to Aktat. "I'd rather do this with you on board. Could you come?"

"Of course." In seconds, the eldest of the Jejod sisters strode into the control room. She examined the ship settings. "You've developed suction. You may need to do a vibrate. Let me check what you have." Bringing up panels, she studied lists. "Let's download this one." She hit an icon and they waited. A moment later, the ship shivered and then they were in glide mode, floating through the canyon and then gaining speed as they left the mountain world of the Jejods.

They shot out of clouds.

"Drop me over Deladar. I'll see you soon." She stood and ruffled Tlalit's mohawk, bent nearly double to press her cheek to the elf woman's.

"Will I?" Tlalit's voice sounded tight.

"You will." She went below, and soon they saw her soar past their viewing windows.

They left Erzon's atmosphere, into the black of space, headed for Prokit's Moon. As usual, for distances, as many as could sat in the viewing room.

When safe, Zami ran back and forth with his toys from the lounge. Vatu or Tik followed him, making sure he was safe. Mnenu came over to Yanda, seated at the side facing the view as the planet disappeared from sight. "Want to get a snack with me?"

Yanda could tell this was more of a "want to talk" invitation and obliged. In the kitchen, they made hot drinks and sat at the table.

"I'm going back to Terlond from Prok," he said, slender, tapered hands wrapped around a warm mug.

She gazed at him a long minute, heart seeming to wedge in her throat. "Have you set up transportation?" she asked.

"Tlalit tells me there will be options from there."

So he'd discussed this with Tlalit and Merne but not her. Until now. She reached and cupped her hand around his. "I understand." What she meant was, she understood that he didn't feel well. But he also meant he wasn't going to make this journey to find her daughter. Who knew how long she'd be searching, after all? They had been distanced on the ship, but it made her sad to think of him gone from her.

His lips pressed in a line with slight upturn. "Not just the distance, Yanda. I think you know that."

"Me and Ilan."

His only response was a lift of one brow.

"We haven't...we aren't—"

He lifted his hand from the cup and slid it into her palm. "You're not to worry. You came to Zotoul and we connected. You had a need and shared something beautiful. I don't think this is the end of it. Of us. But you have other needs now. I understand that."

"So, I just go around using whoever I need?" she asked, pushing her voice past a pressure in her throat that had shifted from sadness to shame.

"Don't treat yourself like that, Yandawi."

Everyone seemed to use that name strategically, to remind her that she was greater than...something. She was Xentu. She'd grown to resent the implications, because she knew so little about her supposed people of origin. Her own blood.

He went on, "You've had to make courageous deci-
sions, use your powers for others. You are not selfish. I
don't see you that way at all. You helped all of us on Terlond. You sacrificed, losing time with your daughter to
draw a great stone—a moon—back together. Now you
have further repairs to make. I would help you but I don't
think I'm the most necessary one for that."

"You're needed by Ash-don. By the Neyla."

Suddenly she felt Ash-don's voice, a vibration in her
sternum, confirming, thanking her.

She studied Mnenu's handsome face, complexion now
lined in a web of pale and dark green where it had been
more even and luminous on Terlond. "And you need your
sea."

He dropped his head, and nodded.

With luck and strategic timing, Tlalit coordinated their
journey with Prok's orbit to be the closest possible. The
creamy moon took on swirls of other colors as they approached—peach and indigo, mauve, and faint gold—as
they descended toward its surface.

Merne and Ilan tested the skies around the moon for
any sign of Qontaqi ships, surprised that they found none.

"They will likely have changed registration details, utterly disguised their identity," Ilan pointed out.

"We just have to be on our guard," Tlalit said, hands
busy on the controls, eyes scanning screens.

Welcomed into the spaceport by mellow-voiced flight
control, the ship settled into its designated spot and the
passengers soon paraded off. Green flowering vines covered the walls of the space station. Inside, bots served

warm drinks and delicacies, sweet treats and savory pocket breads. Puffy couches in the shapes of fruits and animals lined walls and center structures topped by distinctive plants. Music, a pleasing blend from various star systems, wafted through. After a short wait in a swift line, they were processed and could enter the city.

Once out of the spaceport, Yanda thought she knew already why Tlalit loved the place. There was something in the air, literally. A sweet aroma gave euphoria. Creativity and open-heartedness were in the structures, murals, even vehicles as she and Zami walked hand-in-hand on the moving ramp that exited through the doors. Chin, Tik, Bonden, Soni, Vatu, Ilan, and Mnenu followed them out. On the street, they found themselves on a rise looking at an intriguing city-scape. Colorful kites fluttered above one section. Buildings had unique shapes, pointed, crooked, convex. They saw rooftops full of gardens, fountains and play structures.

Zami pointed out birds and monkeys flitting or climbing in trees in sun-filled upper stories, open to the city. Yanda was rethinking the plan to go off with Ilan and get trained. She hugged Zami as they stared in wonder with the others. Smells were exotic and sweet. No fumes. The air must be filtered or no exhaust fumes were allowed. Or both.

Tlalit and Merne caught up to them and showed the way to a large town square extending onto lawns. Yanda recognized the stage with performers from Tlalit's vid she'd seen in the bunker on Terlond. Musicians played now. Maybe every day. A crowd picnicked, danced on grass of many hues stretching out into the distance.

Yanda sensed Ilan behind her as they walked. She picked up Zami to let him see more. As they passed an open-air market full of bright produce, cheeses, and herbs hanging from broad carven rafters, Tlalit suggested, "Let's pick up food and eat on the commons."

Zami squealed at the birds that flitted through. The group wandered among bins and displays, choosing cheeses, breads, olives of many cultures, some Yanda had never encountered, others they'd missed on ship board.

At checkout, Tlalit and Yanda split the cost, while others contributed, donating with universal currency. They spread cloths on a hillside facing the entertainment and watching the diverse myriad of off-worlders enjoying the scene.

Zami grasped her shoulder and pointed to a children's area.

"Should we eat a little, then explore those caves and climbing structures?" she asked him.

He nodded, eyes round as little moons.

The group pulled out delicacies from their bags, backpacks and carryalls heaped to one side. Tlalit stepped away to book villas and order transportation. Yanda heard her also making sure her ship had cleared inspection.

Ilan propped his back to a tree and chomped on a stuffed pocket bread. "Are you avoiding me?" he asked Yanda in mind-speak. "Your thoughts seem closed off."

Mouth full, Yanda pulled her eyes from an acrobatic performance on the distant stage and glanced over at the tall man, legs propped in front of him. Red-gold stubble shadowed his cheeks that were usually clean shaven. It caught a lowering sun's rosy rays. He looked attractive to her, suddenly. Had he before? She wasn't sure. "I didn't mean to shut you out."

"Do you want a day or two to play with Zami in this

fun town?" he asked. "There's a lot to do, and you could use a break, I'm sure."

Yanda gazed for a while at the stage, pondering. He seemed to have read her earlier hesitation about leaving the group to work with him. Finally, she said, "Zami can have as much fun with Vatu and Tik. I want to focus." It wasn't just learning to protect herself and what she knew that was on her mind. She thought if she and Ilan could get off together and concentrate, with his skills, she could obtain answers. He knew something about her parents. They were somehow connected to that moon in Unknown Space, maybe the sister moon Ash-don and Shalt had lost. There was something about that dark material that came from Bonden, too. Did he know something more about that? Was it related? "Could Bonden be with us?" she asked suddenly. Bonden was from Ilan's planet. She had survived Qontaqian attack. She had had that evil smoke in her. Was it evil?

Ilan stared away toward the stage. In his shades, it was hard to tell what he saw, what his feelings were. He took a moment before saying, "I think that's a great idea. No one else, though."

No one else. Did he mean Mnenu? Vatu? The healers—Chela, Soni, Shouma?

Regardless of what he meant, Yanda agreed. "We could call healers if needed."

"Yes. Good. I found a place."

Already? Yanda squinted at him. His face was unreadable, chewing, staring at the stage.

She'd forgotten the goodies she'd selected, and Zami, eager to play. Quickly she gobbled some fruit and slices of a plant-cheese on crackers. "Let's go, little monkey." She stood and swept Zami into her arms, heading for the kids' play area.

Tik leapt up and followed. By the time they reached the gate to the colorful playland, Vatu, Mnenu, and Ilan had joined them. Tik launched onto climbing structure and perched at the top. Mnenu and Vatu headed for slides into a pool.

Zami wanted to go on a swing like they'd never seen, in the shape of a lion. After, he chose a spinning top. Yanda, Zami, and Ilan climbed on. Yanda watched to see if it held up under the big man's weight. Ilan winked at her, clinging to the middle as several others climbed on and started it going around.

After a while, they returned to gather the meal and their belongings, and climbed higher on the hillock. Sunset painted the horizon cerulean and lavender. A salmon-colored moon appeared.

"Which is that?" Ilan asked.

"That's our planet, Erzon," Tik said, grinning.

"Oh, sugar, that's a pretty sight," Yanda said.

"Anyone not have accommodation yet?" Tlalit asked.

"You staying on the ship?" Yanda asked her.

"Oh, no. We have a favorite cottage in the hills." She smiled at Merne.

Vatu said, "Tik and I picked something out."

"Couple days. Then I'm going home," Tik said.

Yanda looked at Vatu, wondering where she and Tik were staying, what she was missing. Vatu thought to her, "Can we take Zami? There's a sweet yard, and an animal sanctuary close by."

Yanda conveyed a "yes", grateful. She'd told Vatu about the training with Ilan.

"Chela, Chin, and I got the place next door," Soni said.

Bonden said, "I'm bunking with Ilan and Yanda."

"Then we're all set. I've got *hopos* waiting."

"All but Mnenu." Yanda looked at him, questioning.

"I'm leaving soon, so I can bunk anywhere," he said.

"Come with us," Vatu said to Mnenu. "There's an extra bed."

"Thanks." He ruffled her head nubs lightly.

They gathered on the sidewalk near the stores. Soon, two driverless dome-shaped cars hummed up to them. As they were about to board, rows of masked players entered the commons. Tlalit watched, eyes intent, body obviously atingle with anticipation. "The nightly *Serenz* begins."

Mummers, Yanda thought. Somewhere in the past, she'd read of the old Earth term, from Greek, masked players, related to satire, dark humor or drama.

More poured in from several direction. Some masks were scary. Zami clung close to Yanda and she pressed his head to her chest.

"Should we get settled and come back?" Merne asked.

"We could. It goes on for hours." Tlalit knew all about it.

One of the taller mummers, with a neon skeleton painted on a bodysuit, drew close. There seemed to be no one behind the eyeholes. A chill ran down Yanda's spine.

"The best part is actually in the Taverna," Tlalit explained.

"What do you mean, best part?" Yanda moved closer to the tall elf.

"Underground," Tlalit answered. "There's a sort of mirror of what's happening here, but it's much more. It goes to other parts of the world. You remember *Withum*?"

Of course, I do, Yanda thought. "Yes."

"It's a sort of AI universal mind-melding," Tlalit went on. "One finds answers,"

"Let's go then." Yanda pulled at Ilan's arm.

He bent to Yanda's ear. "You have to be careful in there."

"You'll be there to help." Yanda smiled tremulously. If she could find out where her daughter was, she had to risk it.

Zami sucked his thumb, a sign that he was upset.

Merne stepped to him and let Tuk-Tuk run onto his shoulder. He perked up, running his tiny fingers along the marsupial's back.

Vatu extricated Zami from Yanda's arms. "I think we'll forego this part of the evening. Soni and Chela are bribing me with promises of bubble baths and facials—whatever that is—with special clays and salts they found in town."

Reluctantly, Yanda let Zami go. As she watched their group, with her son, climb into one of the cars, she waved, thinking, "Just as well. It doesn't seem like a place for a child," though she longed to giggle and chat about a facial, snuggle with Zami, and read him a story.

CHAPTER

14

Yanda and Ilan, Merne and Tlalit, Chin, Tik, and Bonden started back down the hillock. Above, Erzon glowed like a moon. A mass of onlookers spread out as mummers passed through. All seemed to hold their breath as a scene unfolded on stage.

But Tlalit led them away.

"Maybe we could just watch a little more of this performance," Yanda said, curious despite the scariness of some of the mummers.

"This is better. We can watch another night," Tlalit responded.

They turned toward a street. A block from the commons, steep steps took them into blackness lit only by a neon red sign. Though it resembled a nightclub entrance, the stairwell felt close and silent as Tlalit leaned toward a heavy black door at the base. After a moment, the door opened inward and they pushed through. Noise and heat struck them first as, after a moment, Yanda's eyes adjusted. Screens hummed and glowed along the walls of the first room, packed with humanoids. A maze of low dividers, indicated by strings of lights, led to various halls and stairways marked by cryptic signage.

Yanda saw through the first layer of walls, into rooms, one orgiastic, another lined with banks of floor-to-ceiling monitors showing patrons seated or lying on the floor on colored-light squares.

"This might be better than the library I promised you," Ilan said, low-voiced. He sensed something out of Yanda's reach: magic-enhanced machine intelligence.

Tlalit stepped to a dispenser and collected round chips which she handed out to Yanda, Merne, and Ilan, keeping some for herself. "Passes for Brend Alley." She glanced at Chin, Bonden, and Tik, brows raised.

"I'm just here to watch over you," the warrior woman, Chin, said gruffly, eying the crowd with misgiving.

Tik's head arced over them, swiveling like a bird of prey, long nostrils flaring. "There's an Erzon room," she said. In long strides, she crossed the main lounge, stepping lightly over barriers, headed for a hallway lit by hot chili pepper lights. Or were they birds? Hard to tell.

Chin, used to sticking with the martial-trained Jejods, looked torn.

"Follow her." Tlalit pushed Chin. "I know you want to guard the youngest sister. What would Aktat say if you lost track of her?"

Chin nodded and followed after Tik, a path parting for the imposing woman with her dark stare.

Tlalit led Merne, Bonden, Ilan, and Yanda in another direction. They entered a hallway that sloped downward.

A twist took them to stair and, at the base, a lift. Three levels down, the halls were deep purple.

A strange sensation stirred in Yanda's belly. She glanced at Bonden. "How are you?"

Bonden, sturdy engineer, had seemed robust during their travel to this moon, and through the afternoon and evening, but now, in the strange glow of mauve lighting, a haunted look had come into her face. The others turned to her as well.

Bonden grimaced at the attention. "I'm fine," she mumbled.

Yanda thought Chela or Soni should have been with them. Knowing surgery didn't mean a vast knowledge of healing, though she'd been learning some.

Ilan rested his hand on Bonden's shoulder and she quirked a half-smile at him. Yanda sensed mind-speak between them and pushed closer to keep the connection clear.

"I feel something predatory in here," Bonden said.

"I'm going to trace it. Let me stay in your mind." Ilan rested an arm around her shoulders.

Tlalit and Merne had climbed onto stools in front of a large screen filled with a hundred small square mini-vids. Yanda wondered what could be found on there.

"We'll do that in a minute," Ilan said, noticing her glance. "Let me just see what…" His voice trailed off.

She followed his mind into Bonden's, wanting to know, yet afraid of what they'd find.

After a moment, he said to Yanda, "Warring factions. I think your parents want to find you but they get caught in Bonden's mind. A barrier, or trap she doesn't know is there. Meanwhile, the Qontaqians are tapping at the edges, trying locate her and your parents. I scrambled that but we need to develop greater protection. It's good Bonden is coming with us."

Ilan pulled Yanda and Bonden along with him, sending a mind-message to Tlalit and Merne. "We're going to our cabin. This isn't working for Bonden right now."

Tlalit turned, eyes filled with distraction, and nodded.

From the lift, Ilan teleported them to the street. The three breathed deep of the sweet night air. Ilan put his hands to Bonden's head. Her spirit cleared as his energy washed through her. She could almost watch the healthy splash cascade down the other woman. Maybe she did see it. Bonden's smile was ragged as the strain lifted from her face. "Thanks."

A *hopo* arrived, this one small, for the three of them. Open to the sides and overhead, with only safety bars, like in a theme park, it trundled up a hill, down another, floating with anti-grav above the plaz-paved avenues. On the side of a second hill, the driverless conveyance pulled into a round drive, stopping near a low cottage, walls covered in bright murals lit by night globlights.

The foyer led into an open floor plan, looking out over a balcony across a valley to a cove.

"This is… Wow." Yanda danced down the hall, past a kitchen area into the domed living room. "Where are the bedrooms? Oh. Here?" She spotted a railing spiraling downward.

From the floor below she called, "I'll take this one." She'd entered a small room with a bed like a nest—perhaps influenced by the Jejods on their mother planet, Erzon. Another smaller balcony took in same water view. A bathroom boasted a deep tub.

She went in search of the others. Bonden had chosen a bedchamber off the living room. She sat at a desk, fingering a gadget. A remote, maybe?

"What's that?" Yanda flopped onto the bed.

"I think it must open the shades, or turn lights on and off." She pointed it at the window and pressed. The window darkened to a peacock-blue. Another press, it shifted to burgundy. "Hmm. Well. Keeps the morning sun out. If I want to."

"Good thing nothing exploded." Yanda turned onto her stomach, chin on a fist. "How are you feeling now?"

"Better." Bonden set aside the device. "We have to seek what knowledge can be had from the Taverna. I don't want to prevent you from finding out what you need."

"You won't. We also have to solve what's left in you from the Qontaqians. Well, your people, but the evil ones."

"I'm not sure they were all Qontaqian. There's something larger, other influences."

"Really?" Yanda thought about her parents. And her daughter. Even the Sinisay of Alland who'd helped with her abduction, probably Seiti's as well. Who-all might be involved? "We have to find out if there's any more toxic stuff in you, and…something Ilan said."

"I get the feeling it's at least partly about you." Bonden quirked a smile to soften her words.

"You think even their taking you in the first place is related to my parents?" Yanda sat up as acid ran into her stomach. "Knowing me caused you that horror?"

Bonden got up and sat next to Yanda on the bed. Not an affectionate woman by nature, she gave her an awkward pat on the back. "How could you be blamed?"

"I shouldn't even be in the world. My Xentu blood makes everyone around me a target, I guess." Yanda pulled her legs up and hugged them, tears pricking. "Maybe that's why Alland, with its love-hate thing about powers, *was* ironically the safest place for baby-me." She pressed her forehead to her knees. "I mean...Alland does keep some things out, by suppressing powers, though really also controlling them, using them I'm sure."

"There's something sick about our planets, yours and mine. High tech, desire for power, secret use of talents by those who don't have them, both hate and envy those who do." Bonden crossed her legs and fidgeted with a small device lined in crystals that she took from her pocket. "You were right to join rebels on your planet. I want to do that on mine."

Ilan came in, catching the last of what Bonden said. "I agree."

"You're already part of an underground, or you wouldn't have found me," Bonden said to him.

He nodded but said no more about that. "Let's do some digging, if you two are up for it."

"I just sat on a ship and then played in Prokit's Moon's commons today, picnicked a little," Yanda said.

"But the past few days have been...rather strenuous." He looked them both over.

"Let's do it," Bonden said. She and Yanda stood."

"Let's go down here. There's another level." He led them past the room Yanda had picked. He'd chosen the base of the house. It, too, faced over the inlet but boasted a hot tub on a veranda that gave onto a yard.

"Oh, I didn't see this," Yanda said, jaw dropping at the thought of soaking with that view in the open air. Maybe under the stars.

Ilan sent her a private mind-message: "You're welcome to share it with me."

Yanda glanced around for Bonden. She'd wandered

down to a miniature maze of rose bushes, lit at night by lights aimed up from the edges of the paths.

Yanda stood next to Ilan. He smelled of fresh soap. His dark-bright red hair was combed back, still dripping where it hung over his collar. She gave him a half-smile. "What digging are we going to do?"

"Get this mess figured out," he said.

"I get the feeling you've already sussed out a lot," she said.

"I really haven't. There's a basement behind this. Bonden," he called quietly, glancing up at the sky.

"Coming."

The three filed back in and down a short hall from the back of a small bedroom. A narrow door opened into a sloping cave of a room, cold, with loamy smells. A single bulb cast pale yellow light.

"I've set the house with AI inside the walls, along with a bit of my own…" He searched for a word.

"Wizardry?" Yanda suggested.

The corners of Ilan's mouth twitched upward. "Okay. I'll accept that. Let me just test it." He dropped cross-legged on a mattress at the center and pulled a device from a shoulder bag.

Yanda and Bonden perched on either side of him, waiting.

He set aside his computer. "Let's lie in a row, touching. I want the least amount of energy used for anything but the battle ahead."

"You foresee a battle?" Yanda asked, wanting to laugh but suspecting he meant it.

"We said you'd get some training. I want you in the middle. Bonden and I both have some specific training that you may need first."

They stretched onto the mattress, Yanda squeezed between the two larger Qontaqians. "Like what?" she asked.

"Like deflecting." Ilan held Yanda's hand.

Bonden's strong, warm, calloused one held the other.

"You have to be heartless sometimes, Yanda. I know you're full of heart, and want only to heal. But there are others with less admirable intentions."

Yanda shot Zami a good night kiss. Snuggled between Soni and Vatu, a children's book, propped in front of him, he sent back a "good night" full of his love. They must have gotten that book in town, Yanda thought, not recognizing it. Her heart swelled with envy and fondness. "Good night, you three," she whispered.

"You're not that far from us," Vatu said. "Let's have muffins and *kaffe* together in the morning."

"If I make it that far," Yanda thought. "Thank you for taking such good care of our Zami," she said back. Reluctant, she let the connection go.

Ilan squeezed, acknowledging awareness of her contact with the others. He'd waited. "Okay. There's a sort of plane we can reach that is everywhere all at once. Maybe even in the Unknown Universe. I don't know if I'd recognize it to tap into it, or if it's safe, but eventually we'll have to. I don't know how to prepare for that but I'll find out. You two are going with me. Nothing can sneak up on you with me, in my mind. We can even go to where those screens look, that Tlalit and Merne were accessing in Brend Alley, if it takes us there. I've noticed a thread I want to follow. I sensed it in that room."

"If that's what made my stomach churn then I know what you mean," Bonden said.

"I suspect it is. Ready?"

"Yeah," said Bonden.

"Ready." Yanda closed her eyes and sensed her mind pulled into Ilan's, a now familiar place. She saw what he saw, which became at first a tumble of thoughts. She held his hand tighter as faces, images, and patterns swirled past. Sensations, sounds, scents, all sifted through. Fully engaged, she seemed to leave her body behind. Data came next. AI helped them analyze. She was a human computer, understanding the substance and its elements that seeped from Bonden. Yet she knew she understood nothing of it, beyond some scientific facts, chemical compounds.

Then they were on that moon where she'd seen Seiti. She saw again oddly shaped mountains, and unusual clouds, or missiles, hovering overhead. Flowers seemed to produce oxygen. Where was her daughter?

She sensed the semi-familiar faces of her parents: cold, spare lines with a kind of beauty, eyes set deep and hard to read. The woman had red-black hair resembling her own. The man's was more blue-black. They wore clothes stiff at the neck, of fine fabric.

Yanda wasn't sure if it was safe to address them directly but did. "Are you there on the moon with no oxygen? In Unknown Space?" she asked.

Instantly she felt enemies forcing toward this connection, fierce, hungry. Bonden froze, and Yanda sensed a fight that convulsed her body. Ilan drove the enemy back. Yanda perceived a charge of energy. Who were they? The bad Qontaqis? Her own Sinisay from Alland? She couldn't tell exactly what happened but was almost sure Ilan removed the sinister presence, smashing any detection by Xentus or Qontaqians, of each other, of her or Bonden. She had a vague notion of how he'd done it, the knowledge wrenched from a new power center emerging in her. She shook, with a fragmenting whoosh of energy that left her drained.

She opened her eyes and realized Ilan had crouched over them, shoving her and Bonden together as he placed his body as a shield. He crouched back to his heels. Bonden curled in a ball, into Yanda's side, heaving sob-breaths.

Soni said into their minds, "Do we need to go to the Flari?" She sounded a pinch reprimanding.

Yanda detected the rest forming the hive-mind.

"Next time maybe all of us should be involved in this sort of thing," Shouma said primly, as she probed Bonden's health from back on Sandu.

Yanda hadn't realized tears streamed down her face until a drop tickled her ear. She rubbed it. "Enough people are getting hurt because of me."

"How can you think it's your fault, child?" Shouma reached out to her, sending motherly affection. "Should I come there?"

"You mustn't," Yanda cried with a sob. "You need to stay free, for your family"

"What about your freedom? Your family?" Shouma asked gently.

Merne appeared in the room. "Come on. Let's be together."

Yanda laughed and hiccoughed. "I thought this basement was impervious."

"I let her in," Ilan said.

"Mm-hm." Yanda cocked a suspicious brow at him.

"One has to leave a trusted connection open, in case one is rendered incapacitated," he said, equally primly.

Merne nodded.

CHAPTER

15

S oon they were all on the *Sarsefi*, there on Prokit's
Moon, abandoning enchanting cabin accommodations.

Yanda scooped Zami into her arms in the healing spa
room where Mnenu was already enjoying a dip. Watching
him dive deep in the healthful waters, Yanda suspected
parting from him would be easier since they'd been distanced in these final days. She was also glad she hadn't gotten intimate with Ilan, though it had seemed inevitable, before they invited Bonden to join them.

Ilan helped Soni set up the specialized tub. He was fas-
cinated by her invention, and they conversed in low voices
about the technologies. Yanda imagined he might contrive
AI applications to it.

Then he moved away and pulled several instruments
from a case. No ordinary case, the sides were covered in carv-
ings tooled into a rich faux-leather. Ah ha! She watched as he

sat, knelt and crouched all around the tub, holding up sensors that sent wheezing sounds.

She'd settled with Zami at the end of Bonden's bed and half-heard Bonden explaining a gadget to the little boy.

She'd gone into the Flari twice before with Bonden. Twice they thought they'd detected what ailed her and healed her. Would it make any difference this time? Was she reproducing the dark smoky substance? What hold did her enemies have? Ilan seemed so capable, and Soni could work wonders. Hell, they had Shouma and Chela, astoundingly skilled in spirit, mind and body healing. What was lacking?

She couldn't think about her parents' part in this now. That mystery was too fraught and ingrained in her deepest psyche.

Merne entered and sorted packets on the counter in Soni's area. She must have gone shopping. Everyone had their roles.

Soni asked Bonden to undress and get in. "The temperature is perfect."

Zami stood up on the bed, hand on Yanda's shoulder. His eyes held a strange focus. She felt a presence, shared with him. His grandparents lurked, hidden yet perceptible. His elven father, Zamani, made himself known. She saw him at an altar in his office deep in the caves behind Shalt.

She'd thought of him lately. What had drawn him? Though in general she avoided him in her mind, just now she welcomed his presence as an ally. They needed new elements in this battle.

He gave Zami a mental kiss, he and his only son spoke briefly, then he said, "I'll come there if you'll welcome me."

"Yes, of course," Yanda said, though she inwardly groaned. Zamani, Mnenu, Ilan. All they needed was Tenali there to make the scene complete. Or completely too complex. She tapped on the hive-mind. "Can I ask Shouma to come here?"

"Good idea." Bonden lowered herself in, expression suggesting pleasure at the soothing bubbling warmth.

Vatu sat by Zami who still stood on the bed, poised, waiting for his father.

Yanda kissed his cheek, then got up and approached Ilan, still crouched by the tub. Squatting next to him, Yanda asked in a low voice meant only for him, "Do you think this time we can finally get the bastards out of her? Were you able to follow them back to the source?"

"I caught some information."

"Are they here on Prokit's Moon?"

"It's a network. Part on Qontaq. It's hard to pin down physical location though I've captured some identifiers. I'm not sure they're staying as much as returning, which means I have to shield her better. But I do want to follow the threads back to their sources, and so does she."

"She's bait then." Yanda grimaced.

"I choose to be." Bonden said from the blue waters.

Shouma appeared, Chela with her. Much more unexpected was who followed: behind them walked Dele.

Vatu brought Zami as she and Yanda hurried to greet their fellow captive fems. Dele, usually aloof, reacted warmly to Zami. She and Yanda had never been close. No one tended to bond easily with the tall, slender Qontaqian. It was hard to reconcile that she shared Bonden's home planet. A skilled flautist, her magical ability was to move objects. Yanda opened an arm, inviting a hug, and Dele bent fractionally to give her a cool brush close to the cheek, then stood away.

Zami studied Dele.

She cracked a rare half-smile. "You've grown quite a lot," she said to him in her husky voice.

"Yes, I have." Zami puckered his lips for a kiss and Dele could not refuse though she quickly backed away again.

"We've got just about everyone," Vatu said.

"Just missing Aktat and Jat," Chela commented.

"I thought you were off somewhere with a lover," Yanda said to Dele. "Is he, or she here?"

She shook her head. "I caught a whiff of the mind-meld. Left him behind. We needed a break anyway. And...Prokit's Moon? I've wanted to come here forever."

Now that was more like the Dele Yanda knew: self-serving. She gave a slow nod with a hint of a smile. "How did you get here? Oh, Shouma. Of course."

Dele nodded. "Not that I don't want to help Bonden. And all—" she waved a vague hand around her— "that's going on."

All that's going on. Qontaqians—her own people—torturing her planet-mate, Bonden. Yanda felt Ilan's warm hand pressed to her back. "This must be Dele," he said.

"Oh, let me introduce you."

"I know of you," Ilan said. He spoke softly so that Yanda did not hear.

Dele at least feigned interest as she held out a graceful hand to him.

The two Qontaqians moved away, discussing their planet's politics.

Yanda didn't know the name references but took in the familiarity of their shared planet of origin. His energy near the attractive woman, famous on their planet, roared like a beacon. Am I jealous? Yanda wondered. *Moons. Grow up.* She realized for the first time that she'd taken Ilan's affection for granted. He must admire this elegant, haughty woman of renowned skills.

Okay, bring head back to the immediate. That wasn't hard. Vatu pressed against her side, wiggling her fingers meaningfully to draw her attention.

"...So, we should take the little guy into the pool?" Vatu sounded as though she may have said that twice without getting Yanda's attention. "Right? Yanda?"

"Oh, yes." Yanda walked with Vatu toward the long lap pool fitted deep into the ship's flooring on this level. "It's something to see Dele again, isn't it?" She checked Vatu's expression.

"I can't believe it. She had a chance to be anywhere. Partying, doing what she loves. She could be playing music on the Prokit stage. Instead, she came here."

Yanda made a face. Why give Dele so much credit? Vatu and the others had helped save Bonden. Yanda had set aside time from her search for her daughter and they continued to do what was needed to heal her. Of course, it was all intertwined.

Tlalit was committing her ship to Yanda's mission. Why? Yanda's gaze wandered around the room, as she thought of the sacrifices they'd all made. Especially Ilan. He'd risked the most. Ilan, who was now hunched a little toward Dele, taking in her every word. What else? Her voice? Her scent? Yanda's heart squeezed. But even as his eyes were on Dele, they let Yanda know he took in her location. *He knows I'm jealous.* Yanda crouched by the poolside, setting Zami down to undress him. "You've had a lot of water lately, Button. What do you think of that?"

"I like it. And when I'm on Terlond again, I'm going to swim in the sea with Uncle Mnenu. He says he'll show me how to swim with the *tesu* all day, go where they go like we live with them. If it's okay with you." Zami pulled off his night clothes. "I'll show you how the *tesu* jump."

"I know you'll love that. I might come along for some of it." Yanda kissed his temple.

He kissed her back and jumped into the water, like a seal already. When he came up, he asked, "Are you coming in?"

"I think I'll probably be joining Aunty Bonden in the tub." She glanced in that direction. Dele no longer stood by Ilan. She had dropped into a poolside chair and was assembling her *zhoun-zhoun*—the Qontaqian flute—from her bag. She rubbed it with a cloth, put it to her lips, and blew sound that was somehow ancient to Yanda's ears, first breathy notes, then a long smooth aria.

Ilan stood still, listening from next to the Flari. Again, a pang hit Yanda. She couldn't enchant him with flute song. Shaking herself, she went down on her elbows to get her face close to Zami's. "I'll come in with you after, 'kay?"

"Okay, Mommy." He turned and swam to Mnenu.

Vatu joined them in the big pool. Yanda walked to the Flari, stripped and climbed in. This time Yanda started out at the other end of the pool so they could talk first. Bonden pulled up her legs to make room.

"I don't think I'm meant to turn…what do you call it--lanten?" Bonden said. "Or I probably would have done it by now."

"You could ask Mnenu. If anyone can help, it's him." Too late, she remembered how he'd helped her transform. It was hard to picture Mnenu making love to the gruff engineer. Actually, Yanda wasn't sure what Bonden liked as far as gender. She'd never seen her take a lover. She and Chela had been close but not that way. Chin's affection for Bonden was obvious. In such tight quarters, there hadn't been a lot of outright displays of intimacy in their Citadel prison room. Besides, with the mind-share they'd developed, lovers would have had trouble keeping private.

Ilan pulled a high stool to the side of the tub. He'd found a music stand somewhere to raise his device to the needed height, several instruments attached, his shoulder bag hanging from the stand with more connections protruding.

Tlalit came into their minds. "Prokit's Moon is perfect for this. The atmosphere is particularly…biddable. I think we'll be effective. Ilan, you need to tell us how to line up our shielding."

"I've attuned the tub walls to the Sarsefi network. I'm set to monitor this time. I think we'll accomplish more." Ilan's face held a weight of responsibility and Yanda's heart went out to him.

Yanda felt like this was it. Ilan was set to know everything, not just about the enemies attacking Bonden, but about her, maybe why her parents abandoned her. Everything. Wouldn't he? Should she be this sure? They'd failed before. Or she thought they had. Would Ilan even tell her all he knew?

"Let's try without going completely under water first," Soni suggested.

"Oh. Then I don't need to be in the pool," Yanda commented, feeling foolish.

"I like to have you in here with me," Bonden said, "if you don't mind it."

"Of course not. It feels great." Yanda rested her head back and let herself enjoy the bubbles and heat.

Dele's music continued. Would it play a part in all this? It did seem to weave a sort of spell into the air.

Shouma and Chela had settled on cots nearby, deep in conversation, waiting to be needed, while Soni adjusted dials and switches. Yanda sent her mind to Zami. She saw him from his own sight, somersaulting with Vatu. Mnenu dove under them.

Yanda pulled her mind back. "How are you feeling?" she asked Bonden. "I mean, what do you think about this next step? Are you confident?"

Bonden sat forward, crossing her legs. "This is it. Do you sense it?" She glanced at the tub walls, then around the room. "Look at all the talent we have here. I'm not an IT expert but my senses are picking up...signals." She narrowed her eyes as if looking inward. "Intelligence is building."

Tlalit pushed through the door saying, "I'm glad we're stationary so I don't have to fly the ship. Let's do this." She caught Ilan's eye, rubbing her hands eagerly. She held the door for Aktat and Jat to duck under the tall lintel.

"That's it. We're complete." Chela hooted a cheer.

The Ten Fems who'd been captive together were all in one place again. Their hive-mind allowed Yanda extra perception. She detected the sentience of the water in the lap-pool. "That really is Terlondian water, isn't it, not just an imitation?" she asked Mnenu in mind-speak.

"Absolutely," he responded, bringing his head out of the water.

"And still it can't fully keep you healthy," she said, almost to herself.

"I want to add that to my study when I get back," he said.

"You must be a little anxious. Your parents, too."

"I wanted to finish this with you, Yanda, help you find your daughter." His eyes were intense. "But you're right. For now, there's something weakening me."

"Maybe you can better help Ash-don to find my daughter if you're back with the stone."

"Could be," he said.

"Do I detect new tiles forming on the inside of the pool?" Yanda asked. "Who's doing that?"

"Dele's music, I think. She—seems to be picking up the essence of the water. I think it will help us. I feel a greater connection with Ash-don and our seas."

Ash-don filled their minds—the three of them, Vatu, Mnenu, and Yanda—with a vibrating chuckle. "I can see you on your spaceship. It's been long since I looked upon such a scene."

"You'll help us?" Yanda asked.

"I want answers as much as you do. Well, as much, that's a...meaningless comparison. Very different, our...needs, longings, circumstances." The stone grew somber, but its aliveness remained.

Yanda addressed the full mind-meld, hive-mind and allies. "Should we form a circle? Or net?"

Ash-don pointed out, "I feel the bodies of water as one. Very potent. Mnenu, voice of the Neyla elves, in the Terlondian pool, and I in our sea. I think you should remain as you are, Yanda. What is that vessel in which you submerge yourself?"

"It's called a Flari," Yanda responded. "Ilan added...tech."

"Mm hm. This AI. I've explored it a bit," Ash-don intoned.

Yanda's hand covered a smile. She brought herself back to the serious nature of their job. "Do you have the Neyla Circle with you?" she asked Ash-don.

Mnenu, at the side of the lap pool, caught her eye and shook his head.

"I don't need them for this," was all Ash-don said. Did the stone miss Mnenu leading the Circle of powerful elven minds?

Merne carried in an armload of cushions. Those not in pools sat in a loose circle between them. Yanda noticed Zami resting his head on Vatu's shoulder. He looked sleepy. She again felt a pang that others were caring for her boy. On the other hand, she was grateful. Vatu passed the toddler to Mnenu while she climbed out. She glanced at Yanda. "I'll put him in Bonden's bed."

Yanda nodded and watched as Vatu dried him and snugged him into Bonden's cot, then slipped on a simple bodysuit and joined the circle on pillows. Zami immediately curled on his side and, eyes closed, sucked his thumb.

Mnenu sat at the end of the lap pool on a shelf.

Satisfied that all were ready, Yanda turned to Bonden, her back in the curve of the tub. "This is it, then," she thought, and gave herself over to the surge of minds blending.

CHAPTER

16

Ilan took the lead. Yanda wondered if he'd ever been in this type of mind-meld, with so many. He'd, of course, done intense mind-work with the others on Qontaq, and even while in hiding on Alland. She knew little about the rest of his life. She felt Shouma guiding, supporting, adjusting as the rest on the ship added their strengths to the mix. Tik, Jat, and Aktat had found perches above in the greenery and crouched, their long thin limbs angling out from foliage.

Ilan suddenly lifted the barrier that had been protecting Bonden. Qontaqian and other energy, now familiar from previous battles, crashed into their shared mind space. Ilan tracked it with AI snares he'd lain all around the Flari and ship, and especially in his ELAC. Yanda and the rest followed the spies' trails through the ship's networks and back to their origins. No wonder Tlalit had looked so smug.

Along with Ilan's mind and understanding, they stuck to the invading energies. Ilan, all the while, shored up his data-feed to track them. They might move or change but he had too much on them now. He had identifiers to pass on to his cohort on Qontaq, to follow up without delay, before the snakes could slither away.

There was something else that had to be followed, he told the mind-meld. Ilan and Tlalit, at their devices, detected connections. Alarms went off in Yanda's mind as Ash-don projected the memory to Yanda's vision of her daughter on a planet in Unknown Space. Like a glimmering thread, the energies led the mind-meld.

Ilan roared into their minds. "Not Unknown Space. I'm getting something back on Alland. Wait."

Yanda held her breath, heart hammering.

"Jelat." Ilan tapped his keyboard. "And Arc."

Yanda groaned. Not Arc. She'd thought him peaceful, kindhearted, uncorruptible.

"No," Ilan assured her. "Arc's been fighting. What?! Goddamn you," he roared.

Yanda realized Ilan was in Jelat's head. They all were. The rest went to a low hum of presence, helping to hold Jelat still, keeping down his defenses as Ilan confronted him.

"Where is she, you stinking *cabreeli*?" Ilan jammed a mental thrust into the other man—baby-faced Jelat who'd presented himself as an ally and nearly given her to the Sinisay, the part of the Allandian government that monitored talent, prevented its use, yet sequestered its powers and probably sold her to Kridenit.

Yanda gripped her hands together, barely aware of her surroundings as her breath came and went in shallow puffs. Images burst into her mind as if obtained against Jelat's will. Of Seiti. On Alland? Had he projected a false vision of her on a strange airless planet to deceive Yanda and send her out across the universe to possible death? "But why didn't I feel her on Alland?"

"She's been completely sealed off," Ilan answered. "There's no way you would have detected her."

"Why didn't I ever read her in Jelat's mind? Am I really so weak at it?" Yanda thought, throat tight.

"Did you read anything in his mind?" Ilan asked her.

"No, not really. Can you detect where she is in his mind?" Yanda could barely breathe now.

Ilan pulled them out of the lines of connection, back to their bodies.

Yanda lurched out of the water and stood. "No! Too soon! We didn't find out where she is!"

"Oh, I'm going to bring down a rain of surveillance like he's never seen." Ilan hunched over his device, oblivious to anyone else.

The others looked stunned as well. Shouma also jumped to her feet. Her face held something way beyond shock. She appeared horrified.

Yanda climbed out of the water. Drying herself instantly, she grabbed her coverall and pulled it on as she ran to the elder. She took her hands. "What is it?"

"There's way more than Alland's Sinisay involved." Shouma's face held a storm of shifting emotions, dark, and personal.

Yanda hugged the older woman who'd taught her to read minds even at great distances and so much more. Shouma stood rigid, caught in a nightmare Yanda could not fathom.

Yanda lay on her bunk, one level down from the pools, Zami snuggled into her, asleep. Tears would not stop flooding, of regret, of self-incrimination, of missing her daughter.

Vatu climbed from above and squeezed in beside her, a comforting arm around her.

Yanda asked, "Will you lie with Button?" She touched Zami, then kissed Vatu's cheek, grateful eyes crinkling at her.

"'Course." Vatu scooted in and let Yanda climb out.

Quickly dressing, Yanda slipped through the door and ran up to the pool room. Not finding Ilan, she descended back to the sleeping quarters and tapped on his door. No answer. Sagging, she descended to the main deck. There she found him, red-eyed, face lit by his device's screen, in the control room.

She dropped into the seat next to his. "What have you found?" She pulled up her legs, hugging them, bracing for what she might hear.

"We'll do better being there." Ilan went on tapping feverishly without looking up.

"Quicker to get there than Unknown Space." That reminded her. "I need to try again to reach Tenali. But Shouma detected others. Not on Alland. Did everyone hear that?"

"No." He sat up straight. "What didn't she tell everyone? What does she know?" He looked ready to go wake the older woman.

Yanda was surprised he'd not detected the same thing as Shouma. Instead of leaving the room, he started typing again.

"Do you think it's Jelat who put a false holograph into my head, of Seiti on that unreachable moon?"

Ilan glanced up. "He might have. Someone must have."

She hoped he didn't mean her parents. Her heart ached, seeing his bleary eyes. "You need rest."

He shook his head. "No time."

"Are your contacts getting the assholes on Qontaq?"

Ilan finally sat back, resting his hands, a smile at last spreading on his face. It always transformed him, even this tired. "That they are."

That was some comfort. Yanda sent a gentle mind-check up two floors to where Bonden slept. She ran a quick diagnostic without disturbing the woman. Ilan detected what she was doing and entered her mind to help.

"Bonden seems clear," he said.

Yanda nodded agreement. She didn't add that she'd seemed clear twice before. She let her tired head drop to the back of the seat and closed her eyes.

Ilan put an arm around her and pulled her to him. She curled into him and tried to push worries away.

Hours later, Tlalit found them, Yanda curled in her seat, Ilan again at his laptop. Yanda rubbed her face and pushed to sitting as Tlalit dropped into her station at her controls.

"I'm gonna go rustle up *kaffe*. Want some?" Yanda asked them both.

"I'd love it." Ilan grabbed Yanda's hand and squeezed it, giving her a crooked smile. "Hope you got a few winks."

Yanda nodded. "I think so." She remembered dreaming so she must have.

In the dining area, she found Shouma, hands wrapped around a steaming mug.

"There's some left." Shouma indicated a pot wedged into a prep module on the side wall.

Yanda helped herself and poured two more. "I'll be right back."

She brought covered mugs to the control room and handed them out, then returned to sit with Shouma, adding nut milk. "Can you tell me now what you detected?" She sipped her hot drink.

Shouma rested a hand on Yanda's. "There are things I haven't told you about my past."

Her eyes held a troubling emotion, akin to remorse, Yanda thought. She shifted, uncomfortable with the other woman's self-flagellation. "I'm sure we both—"

"No. Not like that." Shouma shook her head, her brown-grey braid swinging with the motion. "My people have history with the Xentu."

Yanda's mood sank further as she discerned the possibility that Shouma had known her past all along.

"Do you know where Chin is from?" Shouma drank.

Yanda's eyes narrowed with the seeming change in subject. She sipped, swallowed. "I don't think I ever learned that." Her voice was low. Though for the most part she trusted Shouma implicitly, secrets had become a plague in her life.

Shouma leaned forward and whispered, "Blaz."

Yanda's head came up abruptly, staring at her elder. "That's... I've never heard of anyone being *from* there."

"I've kept her secret."

"It's in the same star system as your home planet, isn't it?"

"Yes. Elznap and Blaz are in the same star system though not close."

"Okay. And?" Yanda got up to fix toast. "Want some?" She held out bread.

"Sure." Shouma stood to get nut-butter and jam made from ship-grown harvests. "Chin's parents were in the service industries of...that place." She glanced at the doorways on either side.

"Is your being captured by Krid mixed into this story?" Yanda asked, waiting by the toaster.

"I won't go into all that. It would take too long."

Tlalit's voice came over the speakers, "Please meet us by the pools."

Shouma and Yanda glanced at each other with raised, questioning brows.

"I guess we'll bring the toast with us." Yanda wrapped the pieces in a warming cloth.

They took their *kaffe* and climbed the two floors. All the crew and passengers gathered in the spa room. Yanda spotted Vatu and took Zami out of her arms. "You two sleep a bit?"

Vatu looked quizzical. "I think he did. I was too busy worrying."

"You could have brought him down and joined us."

"I figured you had serious talking to do," Vatu said quietly, warm concern in her eyes.

"I did." Yanda kissed the blue Mingal's head. "Thank you for snuggling this guy."

Zami rested his head on Yanda's shoulder as she looked around at the many familiar faces in the fifty-foot-long spa room, half that in width.

"Hi everyone," Tlalit said to the group. "I gathered you together so we can make plans."

Before the ship captain could go on, Yanda stepped next to her and faced the rest. "I'm going to hop to Alland with Merne and Ilan. Mnenu—" she swallowed over a tight lump in her throat— "I'd like you and Zamani to take Zami to Rotoul. I'll come there as soon as I have Seiti."

Vatu stared at her. "But—"

"I'd love for you to be with them, Vatu," Yanda said. "Zami is used to you. And he adores you, of course."

"I'm sorry to contradict, but I think we should all go to Alland on the *Sarsefi*." Tlalit crossed her arms, magnificent cockatieled head arched back. "It's all of our fight. You need us."

Yanda had assumed the elves would want to return to Rotoul. "Thank you. But it will take weeks in the ship. We need to go first." Yanda pressed her cheek to Zami's. He squirmed to look at her. "It's best for you to spend time with your daddy, little man, in the elven forest where you can swim and climb and—"

Zamani stepped forward out of the crowd. "Mnenu and I will take him h—"

He'd started to say "take him home" and her stomach roiled with the unending threat of losing her son.

He bowed his head, emotion ripe in his usually unreadable face as he stepped toward her.

Zami pushed up in her arms, head turned toward his papa.

"Okay." She kissed his soft cheek and let Zamani lift him from her.

The Elf and his half-Elf son pressed foreheads, sharing thoughts. Such a rich tie they'd had since Zami's conception, Yanda knew, throat constricted. How often were they in touch? She didn't even know. She turned away. "Can we get ready?" she murmured to Ilan, unwilling to watch the scene of devotion any longer.

Shouma stepped to her and said in a low voice, "I can transport as well."

Yanda realized she could. She'd love to spend more time with the elder healer, and needed many more answers from her. The powerful woman of the Sonda race seemed ready now to tell her. "You want to come to Alland with me?"

"You might be facing far harder odds than we did with Krid."

Ilan moved closer, his heated chest against Yanda's shoulder. She was glad for his presence. She said to him in mind-speak, "Shouma thinks Blaz might be involved. Did you detect that, too?" If he said yes, she'd have once again been deceived in how much he knew. But his brow creased in confusion.

"I'm going to fill you in on all I know," Shouma said, expression determined.

"That'd be nice." Yanda's mouth twisted. She didn't add "...for a change" though the thought hung in the air. She felt half-guilty even being angry with the woman she revered. But fury bubbled up. She was just starting to register the immensity of what the woman had kept from her. Her cheeks heated as she thought of the other woman looking into her eyes, working deeply with her mind, and never, ever telling her what she knew, what she needed to know. Would she even tell her now?

CHAPTER

17

Ilan put a hand on Yanda's shoulder. Its heat washed calming energy through her. Yet she was tempted to shake it off, not feeling able to accept comfort. Then she slumped, giving up. "Should Shouma come with us?" she asked Ilan. She noticed Merne, several feet away, glancing toward them as she spoke with Soni and Chela.

"I think we'd be very lucky to have her," Ilan said. "Especially now that I know there are elements tied to her people, connecting to yours..."

Yanda sighed in resignation. To Shouma, who'd kept answers from her, she said, "I'll be grateful to have you with us, if you're willing to come." She thought about the woman's age, and the fact that her family was elsewhere, in another star system. "Am I right to send Zami away from me?"

Shouma said, "I know it's hard." She took her hand in hers. "But it is best."

"What kind of a life is this?" Yanda choked.

"You're fighting to make it better, for him and for many others." Ilan laid an arm around her. "And he has others who love him. He's lucky for that."

"Maybe he should come to Alland. I can't stand the thought of losing both my children." She looked around. Holding his father's hand, Zami was showing him the lap pool, jabbering away. Zamani cocked his head, listening intently, asking questions. Tuk-Tuk perched on Zami's shoulder. The boy's tiny hand stroked the primate. Yes, he'd be fine, she thought with a pang.

Merne came over. "When are you thinking of leaving?" Before they could answer, she asked Ilan, "Have you thought about where we should land?"

"I've been considering." He led the way to the door.

Yanda and Shouma followed.

On the stairs, Ilan elaborated, raising the merits of the city of Skarth, also parts of the countryside where the rebels had hidden. He turned to Yanda. "But then there's Pedore. That's a formidable fortress, and has the crater. You think Arc is a staunch ally, don't you? I think so, too. And Cillen. But maybe we should have Soni with us if we go there."

"It seems to have become a stronghold of the Sinisay, with Jelat's help," Yanda brought up bitterly. "I don't think we can go there."

"That's where answers are then."

Yanda said, "That's true. We can ask Soni. She seems reluctant to return. And do you think Bonden's okay without her? What if she has a relapse?"

"She's been teaching Chela about the Flari. But honestly, I think we have made Bonden safe."

"Still, if she wants to stay with us for a while, I'd love

to have Bonden with us there as well," Yanda said.

"It's starting to be a big group. But maybe that's what we need," Merne said.

From the base of the stairs. Yanda sent mental feelers up to Soni.

"What's up?" the brilliant, freckled healer answered in mind-speak.

"Would you like to go to Pedore with us?" Yanda asked, feeling a smile creep onto her face. "Maybe take it back?"

"Would I!"

Soni appeared at the top of the stairs and sped down to them, canvas satchel bumping at her side.

"You packed that fast?" Yanda asked, laughing.

"It was ready."

"Okay, I guess there's not much holding us." Yanda glanced around at the others.

"I'll gather my few things," Shouma said, pressing the button to open the sleeping corridor.

The five—Ilan, Yanda, Merne, Shouma and Soni—said their goodbyes upstairs. Yanda didn't want Zami watching her disappear so they'd met up in the lounge by the control room. Soni suggested the caves surrounding the crater. She knew of a deep labyrinth where thoughts and mind-registers could be hidden from even the most powerful of sentients or psi-wielders.

"And there's a hideout," she added. "A refuge from the refuge."

"Really?" Yanda thought about all the secrets enfolded into every place she'd ever known, or thought she knew.

The group held hands. Darkness roared with inner activity and then they stood in a new place filled with unsettling smells of close wet earth, and the sensation of many feet of ground overhead. Water dripped somewhere in the fecund silence. Yanda reeled, reached for a wall as she sought her bearings. Her hand touched raw hardpacked dirt. She built a float globe to see where they were. A tunnel stretched in both directions.

"Come this way." Soni led a short distance and touched the wall. An opening appeared. She stepped through and brought up lights that appeared green, the length of a long room with tables down the middle filled with plants growing. It was an indoor garden. Cupboards lined the walls and there was a kitchen area to one side. Fresh air filtered in. She recognized the netted ceiling allowing in light but hiding their location.

"Few know about this place, even among the Pedoreans." Soni opened cupboards, revealing an extensive stock of sealed foods. "A few of us always prepared for this time."

"Does Jelat know about it?" Yanda asked.

Soni turned toward her. "No." Color rose in her cheeks.

"You suspected him early on?" Yanda walked to a raised plant bed and touched a vibrant leaf, wondering who tended them as she braced for Soni's response.

Ilan stepped between them. "They had to go along, Yanda, knowing you were coming to me."

"You were trying to catch him? Reveal him? Zami and I were a trap?" Yanda brushed a hand lightly over vegetable fronds, her heart racing, stomach churning.

Soni and Ilan shifted, uncomfortable.

Shouma came to Yanda and slipped her hand under her arm. "Let's let the stories unfold, bit by bit," she suggested quietly.

"I'll make something hot to drink." Soni busied herself heating water, pulling jars and cups from shelves.

Ilan laid out his portable device on a side counter and took a stool.

"Are we definitely shielded?" Yanda asked.

"Yes. We're safe here." Soni brought folding chairs and set them around a firepit where she raised an ambient flame to warm them like a hearth.

Shouma squeezed Yanda's hand. "Let's sit. I want to concentrate on screening for any awareness."

Yanda was glad to have Shouma's motherly presence there. For the moment, she let anger and hurt, sense of betrayal, all settle to a low simmer. "Where do we sleep?" she asked Soni, accepting a cup of herbal tea. She felt a yawn coming on and realized the trip had tired her. Plus, she'd slept little the night before.

Soni went to the far wall and pulled out a built-in sleeping platform that had appeared to be another cupboard. Yanda saw them all along the wall, extending out of sight.

"Tricky. This could house quite a few refugees. Have you stayed here before?"

Soni sat with her cup. "Oh, yes. I'm one of the Keepers."

Yanda's brow quirked. "Are you sure you kept it from Jelat? He's a clever guy." And sneaky as hell, Yanda thought.

"Yes. I'm certain." Soni blew on her tea, then sipped.

Yanda thought she'd have a bite to eat, then sleep, but when Soni fixed pocket bread sandwiches, Shouma invited

Yanda to take one and come with her. They walked to the far end of the room where a small fountain splashed into a pool at the center of a walking maze, rocks marking spiraling paths. Ferns and flowering plants lined the edges and there were benches by the water where they sat.

Shouma took a bite of her stuffed pocket bread and chewed. Yanda tasted it as well, and waited. Was this a moment of truth?

"I left Elznap under...duress," Shouma began.

Yanda waited, munching sprouts, olives, plant-meats and cheeses, accented by toasted sesame sauce.

"The Sonda—my people—having powers, draw...attention, and envy. Greed. Political pressures." Shouma sighed deeply, then took another bite, chewed and swallowed. "I didn't always agree, even with my own family. After receiving vaunted training, I was asked to do a...mission. I couldn't condone it. So, I had to leave to avoid performing it." She'd been staring at the play of water shooting up and scattering over the pond. Now she turned pained eyes to Yanda. "I don't know the full story of your being placed on this planet, but I know my family had something to do with your parents disappearing." She took Yanda's hand. "That moon where you saw your daughter, it exists. And the smoke that came out of Bonden? I know something about it. It has to do with that moon, and how the Xentu survive there in Unknown Space."

"But the Qontaqians were using it—" Yanda protested.

"I suspect it can leave a trail. It can be used to control, or to reveal, depending on who wields it. The material has...powerful properties. That's why I suspect either a Sonda or a Xentu was involved in Bonden's capture." She set aside her half-eaten sandwich and wrung her hands miserably.

"That *is* disturbing," Yanda said. "But then—"

"Your daughter. Yanda, I'm sorry to say this but I don't feel her here. Ilan has everyone searching—"

"Why did he think she was, then?" A sob burst from Yanda as she stood and paced. "Do you think she's on the missing moon after all? We came the wrong direction? And the *Sarsefi*! They're on their way here. For nothing. Or for…what might happen?"

"It may not be the wrong direction." Shouma again stared at the water, her hands rubbing agitatedly. "But there are things to do here."

Yanda came back and sat facing the older woman. "Tell me. Elznap?"

When Shouma remained silent, Yanda's eyes widened. "Blaz? No, not—"

Shouma's eyes met hers. "There are enslavements there. Whoring, trafficking, dirty streets, mazes of iniquity and crime, torture. But I've heard of a sophisticated school, little known because of the power behind them."

"Don't say. Don't—" Yanda brought up both knees and pressed her hands to her hot cheeks.

Ilan and Merne approached and took a neighboring bench.

Yanda brought red-enflamed eyes to meet Ilan's. "No." She could only shake her head.

"We should tell the *Sarsefi* to keep on. But they can't go directly to Blaz." Ilan held Shouma's gaze.

Yanda wondered fleetingly how much he knew.

Shouma gave Merne a long look. "I know what you're thinking. Elznap. That's on the way to Blaz."

Yanda assumed they'd shared much of Shouma's story, back on Terlond when the two had grown close, during and after the rescue of the fems from Krid's Citadel. Much more than she'd shared with the Ten. Or at least with Yanda.

"I can't… I don't really have a relationship with them anymore." Shouma wrung her hands again.

Merne said, "You'll have to face the music sometime. You have nieces, nephews that you've never met."

"I haven't told you all the story." Shouma stared at Merne.

"Do you want to now?"

Shouma took a long breath, sitting up straighter. As though dragged from her, her voice came out hollow, different than Yanda had ever heard it. "I had to steal to get away. I had to…commit crimes and…hurt people. I'm not sure what-all damage my escape caused."

"You were going to cause damage if you did as they demanded," Merne said, confirming Yanda's suspicion of how much the elf-woman knew.

Ilan glanced from one woman to the other. Yanda suspected he knew some of it, had at least researched. He clearly knew more than she did. Sometimes she would pin down what Shouma knew of her birth parents, but Seiti was the point now. "When did you know my daughter is on Blaz?" Yanda demanded. "Was that why you were starting to tell me about Chin's origin? But then why did we come here?" These bursts of partial news were wearing Yanda's patience.

Ilan leaned forward, hands clutched between his knees. "We have to plan, and we have to find out more. There's a lot involved with your placement here on Alland, tied with Bonden's capture. Shouma says it relates to the

Sonda and the Xentu. I'm inclined to believe that. We can't go bumbling onto Blaz without arming ourselves with relevant information. And some of it is here. Some of it can be pounded out of Jelat, I imagine. But there are others he's connected to who are probably more important."

Yanda gripped her hands and glanced around at Shouma, Ilan, and Merne. A powerful trio.

Soni stayed at the other end, busying herself with clean-up and projects of her own.

"Is it truly safe in here?" Yanda asked the three. "Are you able to test?"

When they'd been in captivity in Krid's Citadel on Terlond, Shouma had been able to search the minds of the spy mages as well as detect thoughts into the city around them. That's how she'd found Merne. Both had formidable reach and ability to sense the presence of others' minds. Ilan did so in other ways. All three nodded.

"I'll set up reverse spying, though," Ilan said.

"Is Jelat here in Pedore?" Yanda asked.

"He is," Ilan confirmed.

"Who else that was in my apartment is on his side?" she asked with trepidation.

"No one." Ilan held her gaze, giving off assurance and concern.

"Are they still in my apartment?" she asked. From the pit of her stomach, she detected a sense of rootlessness, that she had no home, no real haven, no place of her own, in the universe.

"They are. They're keeping it safe." Every inch of Ilan seemed to yearn to move closer to her, to give her reassurance with his touch. All the cells in his body and mind broadcasted that to her, and to the others.

Shouma's eyes moved between them, briefly amused, but they returned to the shadowed look of worry. Ilan observed this and sat back, also returning to business. "We begin the process of tracking, and we won't make a move till we know Seiti's location. That'll be mind-search and AI. We'll start—"

Yanda's bones registered the rumblings of Ash-don and Shalt. She immediately shut out the conversation around her, as if by imperative, and concentrated on the stones.

"We are not bothered by some of what would keep you out of Blaz's internal workings," Ash-don told her.

She thought the Stones were probably reaching Mnenu, Zamani, and Tlalit on the Sarsefi as well. She invited them into the mind-meld with the stones. "What do you detect on Blaz?" she asked.

"We will focus there and tell you when we know," Ash-don conveyed in that way that seemed to vibrate in her bones.

Then a mental register she hadn't detected for quite some time—months—came into the mix. Tenali. Her breathing quickened. She couldn't deny the love that still lurked. They had shared an attunement possible only for those who had similar deep wounds from childhood. She saw Merne swell at Tenali's presence in their mind, then flinch at these thoughts of childhood wounds. It couldn't be helped.

"Where are you?" Merne and Yanda asked at once.

His mind-signal was weak, staticky. "On the edge. I've been researching how to enter Unknown Space. Mingalean scientists know something about it."

"You've spent time on Mingal?" Vatu asked, joining the mind-meld from the *Sarsefi*.

Yanda realized how many must be in this sharing of minds.

Tenali said, "Mostly...shared documents...vids. I'm not much...wet living spaces." Tenali's messages crackled through, half-obliterated.

"Be careful, son," Merne said.

Tlalit asked, "You're converting your engines to enter Unknown Space?"

"I've added alternates I can switch to," Tenali explained.

"We might not need to go there," Yanda said, wishing she could talk alone with him. "Seiti may be closer." She hesitated to share too much, even though she'd been assured of the privacy of their communication in this underground space.

"Are you sure?" Tenali asked.

What did he know? She longed to be with him, to talk about everything deeply, not in this broken, fuzzy manner. She turned eyes to Merne and asked privately, mind to mind, "Can we go to him?"

Ilan stared at her, clearly against that idea. Not so private after all. The Qontaqian had formidable mind powers, and could be brazen when it came to Yanda.

CHAPTER

18

That evening, the five settled sleeping arrange-
ments and waking shifts; someone had to monitor
random thoughts that might become vulnerable
in sleep. Soni took the first.

Yanda carried her toothbrush into the small bathroom,
relieved to enjoy a moment of relative privacy. She sent
thoughts to Zami on the *Sarsefi*.

He heard her immediately and responded. "Da and I
are going to Rotoul."

Her stomach clenched, but he seemed happy. She gave
him virtual kisses across the lightyears.

When she came out, Ilan approached her and rested
his hands on her shoulders. "If you wish to go to Tenali and
resolve…what you need to, I'll stay here and find out what
I can." He spoke softly, as others settled into piles of quilts
on their sleeping platforms.

She appreciated his offering, which released her some

from guilt. "Let's see what the Stones say."

He nodded and let his hands drop. They went to their allocated beds, his some distance from hers. That was just as well, she thought. She snuggled under her covers. There was a dynamic connection between her and Ilan, always on the verge of more.

As she drifted off, she felt Zami crying, asking for her. She let her spirit travel to him and wrapped spirit-arms around him. "We'll be together soon. I'm going to make everything safe for us." How soon though? She didn't know.

He accepted her love, coming though it did in spirit-form only, and settled.

Lights dimmed; only a few low strips gave an ambient glow. Yanda let her lids ease shut as she listened to others breathing, and a few low murmurs of conversation. Smelling plant life, and soothed by the quiet murmur of the fountain at the far end, she eventually slept.

Sometime in the night, she woke to the Stones rumbling in her bones, tickling at her mind. She sucked in a breath. "What?"

"It's yes to both," Shalt said.

"Huh?" Yanda sat up and scooted her back to the wall. She rubbed her eyes, trying to transfer from dreams to mental brightness.

"Yes, you have to go to the ends of the universe, and yes, you have to deal with the Blaz," Ash-don declared, in a voice that hummed along her limbs as much as in her mind.

Shalt said, "We have another mission for you."

What the hell? The tone of Shalt's demand sent fear into her stomach as she remembered the last time he'd called to her, which had led to a year and a half of imprisonment. "What's that?"

"You will get your parents to bring our sister moon into orbit around Terlond."

"Oh, is that all?" She wasn't sure if sarcasm registered for the Stones. "So that's definite? Seiti's on Blaz?" It was starting to seem confirmed by all.

In the morning, Yanda shared what the Stones had asked of her. Soni, Merne, and Ilan stared with varying degrees of disbelief, but Shouma only nodded, picking at a muffin.

"These are yummy," Yanda mumbled around a mouthful, then gulped hot *kaffe*. She curled her legs in a robe she'd found in a storage closet. "Is the heat of baking any issue with us being detected?"

"Luckily, since the oven draws from ambient energy in nature, the warmth is also reabsorbed into the ground, undetectable," Soni explained.

"Blaz first then." Ilan hadn't forgotten the original discussion.

The others snickered. One had to find humor when faced with two such terrifying tasks.

Ilan gazed at a message on his screen, *kaffe* in one hand. "The *Sarsefi* has to make a decision now, come here or head toward Elznap."

Yanda looked at Shouma, who for once wouldn't meet her gaze. Yanda turned to the rest. "I think we'll do the research here. They should go on to Elznap. Shouma, will you get them an introduction with your people? Maybe that cousin you trust?"

Elznap was a closed society. Having the powers of the Sonda made tight security necessary, and possible. Yanda had done some research in the sea elves' extensive library. She and Vatu had looked up Shouma's world together and read about the Sonda—S'onda in their native language. She already missed her sweet Mingalean companion.

Shouma again wrung her hands but stilled them and sat up straighter. "Of course, I can." Signs of aging had settled in overnight—tinges of graying in her skin, bags of worry under her eyes.

"Someone is trying to reach you," Ilan said, already messing with his device at the table.

"Me?" Yanda asked.

"Your friend, Beri?" Ilan said.

Yanda got up to look over his shoulder. "Where is he? Last I knew he had a lover he couldn't part from. Was that on Sandu, Shouma?"

"He's being very secretive about where he is," Ilan said.

Ilan had been instructing Yanda regarding how their mind-melds could overlap with AI, what some people preferred to call manufactured neural networks—MNN. "I'll put you onto a channel with him and...is it *Grizzly*?"

Was Beri back with Gisli? Last she'd heard, he was with a lover on Sandu, waiting for a ship back to his home planet. She snorted at the mangling of their friend's name, the quiet Tellotian. She was sure Ilan would get along well with another brilliant IT engineer. "I think you mean Gisli. Now?"

"I think now is a good time, before we lose them."

Yanda took a seat next to Ilan, curious, excited. She'd missed Beri and Gisli. She watched Ilan tap in strings of code. "They're already off this line."

Yanda sighed, disappointed.

"I'm sure he'll get in touch again when he can," Ilan said.

Yanda got up, kissed his short red hair, then paced. So much to worry about. As she wandered the length of the garden tunnel, she sent her mind out to the *Sarsefi*, to her son.

"Mommy," he responded.

"Sweety," she said, expressing affection in her thoughts. "Are you still having fun with your papa?"

"Yeah. He likes to swim, too. He and Uncle Mnenu play with me in the pool."

"I bet they do." Yanda felt Vatu's presence close by and tapped into their mind share. "Hello, friend. I miss you."

"I miss you too. It seems we are heading away from you, to Shouma's home planet, Elznap."

"Oh, good. She said she was sending a message, an introduction to one of her relatives."

"We've received a proper invitation from the leaders. The Laprel dynasty or something."

"Well, well." Yanda was silent a moment. "Be careful though. They're master game players, so I've heard."

"I won't be talking to them. Tlalit knows about that. She's pretty masterful herself. But I think we're getting permission to be in their airspace."

"Right. And to get protection coming there in case the Blaz notice you in their star system. Better if they don't. Maybe Bonden should have come here with us."

Vatu said, "I know you're worried, so far from your son. How are you?" Vatu asked.

"We're in a garden tunnel outside of Pedore."

"You're safe there?"

Yanda could see Zami through Vatu's eyes, playing with Zamani and Mnenu. The elf men's skin was wet and glistening. Zamani's green and brown like lichen on a tree, Mnenu's more brilliant since spending extensive time in the pool. He dove and lifted Zami from his cousin, shooting into the air with him. They came down, swimming deep and launching back up in an arc.

She felt glad her son was learning ease with the water.

Ilan called to her. She broke her connection with the *Sarsefi* and hurried to Ilan.

"We're going to meet Jelat," he said.

"Where?"

"On the far side of Balyou."

"Are you sure it's safe? What if he follows? Puts trackers on you?"

Ilan gave her a disappointed look. "Please. This is me you're talking to."

"So humble." She grinned, hand on his shoulder. "And? What are we trying to accomplish?"

"You don't have to go, Yanda." He turned to her and took her hand. "I know how much he hurt you."

"All of them did, as far as I can see. And how do we solve anything just talking to him? Don't we need to shake them up, clear them out of Pedore?" *Can Ilan do that alone?*

Ilan caught her thought. "I wouldn't be alone. Cillen and Arc are loyal. And so's Soni." He glanced at the healer inventor. "You're right. We should go in there and shake things up. But maybe not before we get your daughter back. Mainly what I'm doing is through the networks. Some of it has already begun." He was silent a moment, checking streams of data on his screen. "It's better if I go with Shouma. Maybe also Merne."

Merne, coming out of the bathroom, heard the last. "Also me what?"

Ilan said, "I know you can pop in and out of places. You can also disguise yourself, right?"

"Can she!" Yanda said, recalling the old woman in the booth in the slum outside of Dondar when they'd first escaped from Krid. She'd out to be a magnificent, lion-eyed elf woman.

Merne came over and sat backward in a plaz seat. "What do you have in mind?"

Ilan wore a crafty expression, eyes twinkling as he imparted the first part of the plan.

Since they were clearly not going to include her, Yanda wandered away. Climbing onto her bed, she opened her ELAC.

The day slid by, with coming and going. Shouma, Merne, and Ilan took several spirit-travel journeys into Skarth, apparently to secret Sinisay headquarters Ilan was tracking down, some threads starting with the attack on Bonden they'd thwarted. Ilan thought he knew now who had recruited Jelat.

Shouma would slide into the minds of possible enemies, they explained to Yanda between trips. Once the duplicitous devil was identified, Merne would read the mind-register, memories and physical being, to be able to emulate him or her.

Meanwhile, Yanda did more pacing. She curled on her bed with her digital device and read. Beri's call made her scramble to sitting. "Where are you?" she asked.

"I can't tell you yet. But I'm going to help you. So's Gisli."

"Tell him hello. Hugs to you both."

Quickly he was gone again, slipping in and out of the ethers before anyone could track him.

Yanda and Soni sat at the table playing Ralashal,

taught to them by Mnenu on shipboard. He'd given Yanda a set of the small shells, painted by Neyla artisans, which she kept in a beautifully embroidered bag in her carry-all.

"I wonder where the three are," Yanda said at the end of a game she lost.

Soni, with her long braids and overalls, could seem all about nature and healing, until she pulled out her portable device and tapped, fingers swift, face concentrating. "There." She shot up an air screen and pointed. Yanda and the others studied lights on a busy, color-coded screen.

Soni finger-expanded a fuzzy red smudge. They saw a building, nothing more. "Well, this is a case where we see the cross-over of mind-meld and MNN." Soni closed her eyes briefly, then tapped on the keys. A new window opened in the upper corner of the screen, showing a map and data streams. "I think they've hit a jackpot."

Yanda watched, glancing from lines of code to Soni's face.

Ilan, Shouma, and Merne appeared back in the room, faces grim.

"Oh, no." Yanda pressed her face into her hands. "Seiti's on Blaz, isn't she?" she asked into her palms.

Shouma came and rested hands on Yanda's shoulders. "We'll get her. At least we know more now."

Yanda stared at Ilan. "This is Bonden all over again, isn't it?"

He scooted a chair close to her. "But we know so much more this time. And I think we'll have help."

"Knowing facts isn't solving getting her back." Drained of any hope, Yanda took her hands away. Blaz was famous for impenetrability. That's why they'd gotten away with being the worst blight in the universe for so long.

"Yes, I think it is." Ilan rested a hand on her wrist on the table. "In my experience, information has always led to solutions."

The others took seats around the table and nodded agreement.

"Did they sense you there?" Yanda asked.

Soni shook her head. "No, I was monitoring. Ilan and the others weren't detected."

Yanda pulled up her legs and hugged them. "Okay. Map it out for me. Give me hope." Her voice was strained with unshed tears.

Merne leaned forward. "This is how we're going to do it—"

"Wait. You do know she's on Blaz?" Yanda asked.

Ilan settled back. "We're not absolutely positive—"

Yanda blew a noise with her lips.

"But!" He held up a hand. "We have found the sources and made headway into their minds."

Yanda glanced at Soni, who held palms-up, as if to say, "See?"

Ilan went on, "We'll be digging further into their minds and we'll get answers."

Yanda got up to pace. "They? Who?"

"That's not important at the moment," Merne said. "We have a plan. Do you want to hear it or not?" She took on her stern, elf-leader voice.

"Maybe not. Just tell me what to do when the time comes. If I have any role at all." Yanda strode away down the room to the fountain.

CHAPTER

19

Yanda dropped onto a bench and cried into her folded arms. The others left her alone.

She sank into dark thoughts that swirled around and around, of her daughter on Blaz with traffickers and torturers. After a while, she heard footsteps.

Ilan sat by her. "We're getting ready to go."

She sat up. "Wait. I thought you were meeting Jelat next."

"We don't need him. We know who's been pulling his strings."

"You do?" Yanda squared her shoulders, ready for a blow.

"It's not important right at this moment." When her eyes blazed, he added, "No one you know."

"You're right," she said. *That* truth could wait. "Are we going to Elznap?"

"Maybe. The *Sarsefi* is already hovering there."

"Beri and Gisli are on Blaz, aren't they? Why else would they be in such danger they have to keep disappearing?"

"Gisli hid under Dondar and followed the networks undetected, so I've heard."

"Dondar isn't exatly Blaz." Yanda's hands clenched 'til they hurt.

Ilan stood. "Time to get your stuff ready."

She was going to see Zami. She jumped up and hurried ahead of Ilan to help pack and clean up.

They heard a deep, rich voice in their heads, calling, "Bring me."

"That's Cillen," Soni said.

"Bring me with you," the plaintive request continued.

Ilan and Soni looked at each other. "It's risky," Ilan said.

"Sounds like she needs to get out of there," Soni countered, eyes worried.

"There are lots of ways for her to get out. She could go to her people in the Outback," Ilan said.

"She wants to help." Shouma and Soni wore determined looks.

Merne nodded agreement. "She and Arc have formidable powers. I've felt them."

"What will happen to Pedore with both of them gone?" Ilan asked.

"There are others," Soni said. "We'll all return, and take down the whole Sinisay."

"Let's fix that situation after," Yanda suggested.

Ilan looked at her impatiently. "We may not get out of here safely if we're detected."

Shouma drew closer to Ilan and put a hand on his arm.

"You and I are capable of shielding this group as we leave."

Ilan obviously felt the older Sonda's immense authority. He straightened, as if he'd been holding too much weight on his own.

Soni and Merne came close to them. They reached out to Yanda who joined them. All rested hands on each other and slipped into a powerful mind-meld.

Shouma spoke as if leading a guided meditation. "We are nothing. Specks on the wind." She breathed slowly in and out; their eyelids drifted shut.

Yanda brought them sight as they slipped through tunnel walls, into Pedore, traveling with their minds into one room after another. They sensed Cillen and Arc in the crater garden, then stood in a circle around them.

"You wish to come help us?" Shouma asked.

"I do," Cillen said.

Arc looked around at the healthy growing plants. Yanda imagined he was loathe to leave the sacred crater unattended. Again, his mind reminded Yanda of sweet nature sounds, a stream flowing over smooth rounded rocks, the rustling of leaves in a low wind. She felt Soni giving him extra coaxing.

He nodded. "I'll come."

And then the two, wiry man and full-bodied woman, both ageless, appeared with them in the garden tunnel.

Yanda grinned at them. "The *Sarsefi* is going to be very full." She hugged Cillen who smelled of sandalwood. She took Arc's hand and he pressed his tan cheek, like fire-warmed leather, to hers.

Shouma announced, "Merne will take you to the *Sarsefi*, Yanda. The rest of us will go to my family's compound on Elznap. For now." She looked like she faced a firing squad, but Yanda noticed something else; there was relief in her stance that Yanda had never seen before, as if she could finally hope to hold her true self and powers with pride.

Ilan looked thoughtful a minute. Then he took Yanda's hand. "I'm going to stick with this Seer for the moment, if that's alright."

Merne and Shouma slipped into one of their private tète-a-tètes, then nodded.

Shouma and Ilan performed a thorough mental sweep of the area, and then the planet as a whole, concentrating intently on the Skarth city area where the Sinisay headquarters were located, while the rest held their minds, giving energy to the effort.

"No one is aware of us or our location," Ilan pronounced, but he made a swift final examination of his AI traps and sync-holes and declared that they had effectively held their anonymity. No one had their focus on this group. They disappeared, headed for their destinations.

Yanda, Ilan, and Soni stood with Merne in the empty lounge of the *Sarsefi*. They looked through to the control room. Tlalit's tall figure sat, back to them at the ship panels.

It took a moment of deep breathing to recover equilibrium after transporting across space.

"Quite amazing, your instant transporting," Ilan said to Merne, who took a small bow.

"You haven't seen the half of it," Yanda said, smiling at the beautiful elf-woman who, turning, strode toward her lover. "I guess the rest are up in the spa room?"

Yanda ran up to the third level, Ilan and Soni following.

From the final stairwell, they heard voices. Yanda raced in first to find numerous passengers. She scanned the faces but didn't see Zami or Vatu. The rest greeted them with a warm welcome.

Yanda noticed Dele stretched languidly on a divan near Mnenu, playing a siren melody. His eyes were on her, mesmerized.

Soni suggested, "Garden?"

"Good idea." Yanda turned.

Soni patted her arm encouragingly. "I'll stay and check on Bonden."

The greenhouse was Zami and Vatu's other favorite place on the ship. Yanda flung herself back out the door and down to the kitchen level. As she pulled open the greenhouse door, fecund smells of brilliant green hydroponics under warming lights struck her. There in the middle sat Zamani, legs folded on mounded dirt, showing Vatu and Zami how to propagate *mantazos*, the banana-like fruit that Elves prepared in myriad dishes, almost as many as mushrooms.

Yanda hurried to the little group and dropped by her son. He threw his arms around her and she drew him close. Vatu hugged both of them. Zamani looked on with affection as a thousand emotions lurked at the back of his dark eyes. Ilan drew up a stool near them.

Zamani unfolded his limbs, brushing off his hands, and reached out to Ilan. "I don't believe we've properly met."

Ilan stood as well. He was slightly shorter than the elf leader, though not by much. "I don't think we have." He gripped the long elven hand with something like reverence, and the two took each other's measure.

Yanda had lived in Ilan's mind several times, most intensely to capture Bonden from her tormentors. She easily joined it now. Though he was accustomed to being a strangely potent force around most people—even among the talents of his home planet of Qontaq—she sensed an inner expansion as he encountered the ancient, refined and artful Elf psyche. The hand-grip lasted moments, while Yanda, Vatu, and Zami watched.

Vatu slipped fingers under Yanda's arm, and they glanced at each other, smiles acknowledging with fondness the immensity of the moment.

Zami turned bright eyes to Yanda. "Papa has been teaching me jumping and climbing. He says he wants me strong for life in the forest. And Mama, the Jejods—" a list of activities tumbled out— "taught me that kind of flying they do. When you jump up way high, you don't need wings. You imagine them. Or make invisible ones. Or something."

She kissed his puckered lips. "You haven't been wasting time. Sounds like you've been learning a lot."

By now, Ilan and Zamani had finished taking the measure of each other and were listening to Zami's recitation.

"Have you been wasting time?" he asked, brows puckered.

Everyone laughed.

"Not really, little one, though others did the bulk of the work. There's still lots to do. We have to make things safe and find your sister. That's what we've been working on."

"Have you been learning, too?" he asked.

The others listened for her answer.

She thought a moment. "I don't think I learned as much as you. But I tried to help."

"Mama's good at helping," he said.

"That she is." Ilan reached down and tussled his hair.

Zamani studied Ilan. "I look forward to learning from you."

"Me?" Ilan looked startled. "What manner of thing could you learn from me?"

"I believe you know quite a lot," Zamani said, face serious at the child's mature words.

Yanda was delighted to see Ilan squirm with pleasure at the praise, though still he seemed a bit baffled, and Yanda wondered what exact skills Zamani had detected.

Meanwhile, Zami sat on Yanda's lap and played with her hair, running his fingers through and looping, as he had when smaller and nursing. She took one of his hands and kissed it. "Do you want to show me where we are? Let's go to the control room."

They paraded out of the greenhouse, through the kitchen and lounge, and into the viewing room.

Elznap's lime-yellow coloration, seen in the near distance, glowed with a pulsing radiance. "Oh. Pretty." Yanda scanned the stars. "Are we within the planet's atmosphere?"

"Not yet," Tlalit said, hands busy on keys. "Shouma says we can land soon. It would be good to replenish supplies."

"I guess they've cleared us to be in their special space," Yanda said slightly sardonically.

"Shouma might want to escape to the ship, if emotions are high with her family," Merne suggested.

"True. I'm curious to see what this planet's like. I wonder if they'll let us get off the ship," Yanda said.

Ilan rested an arm across her shoulders, a grin twitching. "I wonder too. I mean, this much security... Maybe the landscapes are made of jade and emeralds."

Zamani's glance took in the affectionate gesture and he caught Yanda's eye. She looked back at the sky, avoiding his gaze.

"More than friends?" Zamani asked in private thought between them.

"No," she answered, then gently shut him out. Any contact with him was too much right now, with the thought of him taking Zami to Rotoul hovering in her gut.

"The Elznap authorities are only going to let us off the ship if we've been approved by their ID scanning so..." Tlalit shrugged. "We may only see the base."

"They're putting us on a military base?" Ilan asked.

"Yes, indeed. They don't want us mingling without approval." Tlalit's lips, a tangerine to match her hair today, lifted in a grin.

"Well, I'm glad they let us this far. Their skies are some of the safest anywhere, so I hear." Yanda let Zami down.

"Come, Mama. I want to show you what Tik taught me." He tugged her hand.

"I think we may need to get strapped in, if we're going to land on Aunty Shouma's home planet." But Yanda let her son lead her toward the exercise bars outside the lounge.

"Watch. I'll be quick."

When they got through the lounge to the high-ceilinged hallway beyond it, they found Jat and Aktat perched on the highest bar.

Zamani and Ilan trailed after and stood behind her. Yanda braced herself for her son to fly. It was an astounding sight. She'd seen him drift down, and float up-ward, but now Zami bent his knees and launched. He lifted into the air in elegant thrusts, as though wings pumped. His legs worked, like swimming. He grabbed the middle bar and flipped on neatly. "You have to learn, too, Mommy," he said, breathing hard. "So we can go all over in the trees in Rotoul, not just to the treehouses."

"That'll be splendid." Yanda glanced at Ilan, who had moved up next to her. His eyes glowed. She knew he wanted to see the elven forest. She wished she could hold his hand, but Zamani stood close on her other side. "Not more than friends," she'd told him. But it was something more. What exactly hadn't become clear.

"Please strap in," came Tlalit's announcement.

They were going to Shouma's planet, the place of the Sonda, some of the most powerful beings in the universe, crafty, and careful. What would be the reception?

CHAPTER

20

As the *Sarsefi* settled onto the designated landing pad at Glaus spaceport, next to Elznap's capital city, Yanda discerned a thrumming force in her mind. She glanced at Ilan to see if he felt the same pounding. "There's some unbearable pressure on my mind. Do you feel it?"

Ilan took her hand. "They're examining us."

Finding it difficult to think, much less speak, she pushed out words, teeth clenched, "By ID'ing us, I thought Tlalit meant they'd check our criminal records or something." She edged up in her seat, unfastened Zami from the seat next to her and pulled him into her lap. He looked utterly calm. "Zami seems fine. Maybe the Sonda inquisitors dismissed him quickly due to his young age." Meanwhile, she thought, "Stay out. I don't want you in my little boy's head."

"They'll be interested in him," Ilan said, brow furrowed.

"I'm sure they took in his talents. But you're right, with few years behind him, there won't be a lot for them to check on."

Yanda caught Zamani's attention and asked, in thought-speak. "Are you protecting Zami from their prodding? Can you tell what's happening to him?"

Shouma, from her family compound, said into Yanda's mind, "I'm monitoring them as they examine all of you, *chochoi*." The elder woman of the powerful *Sonda* people had sometimes called her this endearment. Yanda had never asked about the meaning, just felt its warmth. She slumped back in her seat with relief that Shouma was watching out for them. Head still buzzing, she asked the elder woman, "Does it always feel like this on Elznap?"

"I imagine you'll grow used to it," Shouma replied. "It's hard for me to discern, having grown up here."

"How's it going for you with your family?" Yanda asked her teacher, mentor and friend.

"Oh. It's been tense. They held a dinner for my return." Shouma conveyed a mix of emotions.

Yanda felt Shouma making a face. She searched for an appropriate response. "How was…was that nice?"

"Aaaaghhh…" was Shouma's mental reply. "I've been imagining something like it for years. Just as well to get it over with. Everyone was there. Absolutely EV-RY-ONE." She gave a small laugh, more a huff. "I ended up promising to get my children and grandchildren to the homestead to meet them."

"They've never—?" Yanda started to ask.

"Never met, never seen. I protected them," Shouma defended.

"Wow, this is something for you."

"Momentous. And I don't know yet if it's a mistake." Again, there was that derisive, barely amused laugh.

"I think the intensity has let off in my mind. It still feels strange here." Yanda moved to loosen neck muscles and saw others in the console room stretching similarly, working shoulder muscles. Zami climbed restlessly around to face her.

"You may unstrap and get up," Tlalit announced, standing and shaking all over to loosen muscles.

"Whoops," Yanda said. "Already did. What's the plan?"

"How about if I come to the *Sarsefi* and we hold a meeting?" Shouma suggested, now including all on the ship in mind-meld.

Merne and Tlalit glanced at each other with grins.

"Told you," Merne said. "She needs a break from family."

Tlalit asked Shouma, "Do you think they won't let us off the ship?"

"They'd prefer not to, curious as they are. Zamani should expect an invitation. Well, probably all the elves. And Yanda. Come to think of it, considering the many talents on that vessel, they may want to keep you all. So, getting off the ship might be the least of your worries." She was ribbing them but Yanda felt profound fear underlying Shouma's words. This was some of the anxiety that had lurked.

"They can't keep us, by universal law," Tlalit said, having pursued legal coursework beyond becoming a ship captain.

"You'd be surprised what they can do, law or not," Shouma responded, then left them.

Yanda, who'd stood with the others to stretch, picked up Zami and kissed his cheek. "How do you feel?" she asked him.

"Hungry." He patted her cheek, then looked around.

As she expected, he was searching for Tuk-Tuk who chittered in Merne's ear. The marsupial scampered across the room and climbed Yanda to reach Zami's shoulder.

"Let's rustle you up something," Yanda said.

Others followed her to the kitchen area. Soon they were preparing muffins and pancakes with what fruits remained on board, taking turns typing needed supplies on a long list.

"Shouma can tell us what fruits are best on Elznap," Vatu said, popping a wrinkled berry into her mouth. Her eyes shone with anticipation.

"That's true. I have no idea what they grow in here," Chela commented.

The kitchen grew crowded. Most of the passengers had joined them to eat and socialize. They continued to scrunch shoulders, loosening tenseness caused by the unusual mind vibrations on this planet of psychics, not to mention the close examinations.

"They'd better provide soothing baths and massages," Yanda said, "considering what they've put us through."

"I agree," Vatu said, grinning.

In the late morning, Shouma arrived at the *Sarsefi's* outer ramp in an aircar and called for entrance. The passengers inside watched as Shouma climbed out with Cillen and Arc. A second, larger aircar landed nearby. A unit in the vestibule examined them for foreign bodies, viruses, and the like before they entered the inner ship. Yanda and others went down to greet them.

"They won't let you into any metropolitan areas at this point," Shouma told the *Sarsefi* passengers," but I want to show you somewhere beautiful. I know you'd like to get out into nature and fresh, non-ship air."

The group nodded eagerly.

"Have Cillen and Arc been able to go into Glaus?" Tlalit asked.

Yanda had been wondering the same thing.

"Only on a very limited basis," Shouma said. "They are absolutely a hit with my people. I think if they stayed, they'd become famous." She gazed around at the diversity of faces in the entry hall. "All of you would. So we mustn't stay long and let them get attached. The Sonda love talent."

Ilan winced, sensing the dangerous anomaly contained in the word "love" in this context.

"You don't need anything. Just come." Shouma gestured for them to follow her.

Eighteen filed out of the ship and onto the transports.

As Tlalit stood at the head of the ramp, hesitating, Shouma said, "Your ship is perfectly safe. I've made sure of that. No one will enter it."

"Damn right they won't," Tlalit mumbled as she set the ramp to close.

There could not have been a more contrasting terrain to Yanda's flat home planet of Alland, crisscrossed with narrow canals but without significant elevation or large bodies of water. The aircars lifted above the main city of Glaus and rose higher to clear dramatic mountains. They passed range after range, with deep, lake-filled pockets, and at last lowered into a canyon, its walls layered in bright hues. They landed next to a rushing river. Yanda stared through transport windows, Zami equally eager taking it all in. The Jejods' world had some steep cliffs and thundering waterfalls, but clouds subdued the color and the soil seemed to all be made of one dark, uniform substance. This land boasted vibrant bounty. On the riverbank, flowering vines shimmered, seeming to radiate energy. Butterflies and darting birds enlivened the scene.

They stepped out onto a sandy beach bordered by multi-shaded grasses. As soon as they'd debarked, the air cars lifted off, rose high, and settled a distance down the canyon.

"Is the whole planet idyllic like this?" Yanda asked Shouma.

"Oh, no. There are blazing deserts and freezing tundras." Shouma smiled fondly.

Yanda thought it must have been painful for her to stay away so long, shunned from a planet she clearly loved. Yanda hugged her elder mentor. "You'll resolve everything. It'll be fine." It was ironic to be comforting the other woman when such dark worries clouded her own mind, wondering how they would get her daughter back, if they even really had tracked down her location.

"It's all of you I'm worried about."

"And your family. Your kids and grandkids. Do you think we shouldn't have come here? We could have landed somewhere else that's also near..." She hated to say Blaz. It had been a taboo place to mention in her childhood, in everyone's. And now her daughter might be there.

"Where else?" Shouma laughed. "The only other inhabitable planet in our system is an ocean world. We'd have to meet in wetsuits, wearing deep-sea diving equipment."

"Some of us wouldn't have trouble." Yanda glanced at Vatu and Mnenu.

"True. I guess you and Mnenu can go."

Yanda said glanced at the sea elf, her former lover who seemed to go everywhere with Dele at his side now. The two were handsome together. She was glad he had found a different focus since she'd been otherwise tied up. Still, she could not deny a tad of jealousy.

"But we need all of us able to be calm, undisturbed," Shouma said.

She was right. In this remote place the intensity of minds lightened. Yanda breathed a comfortable sigh. After a light but sumptuous brunch, Shouma settled cross-legged on the sand. To the group, she said, "Let's have a meeting."

They arranged themselves in a large circle. At the center, the sand shook and then was displaced slowly by a black, shiny dome.

Shouma spoke in a commanding voice. "My people, the La'prel clan, have a very old lineage on this planet. This canyon is under our protection."

Yanda noticed a shimmer above and thought a secure curtain covered over them, like the elven sphere.

Ilan crouched forward, drawn toward the thick dark glass of the dome, its glossy surface with something emanating from it. Yanda reached out, gripping his ankle to hold him back.

Shouma shook her head. "He senses it. Yes, it is a mix of AI and other powers. I have a stable connection with Beri and Gisli set up below us. I can't take all of you. Ilan, Yanda, and Merne will accompany me down. The rest of you, please maintain our strength. Allies surround this area."

The mind-meld swelled in agreement.

Yanda kissed Zami, leaving him held by Vatu, and the four stood.

Suddenly they stood in a chamber below the river beach. As her eyes adjusted, Yanda saw that the walls appeared alive, as though they breathed in barely discernable pulsing veins. The air was close though not stuffy. There was a distinct smell of underground, as in tunnels but under their feet was a soft carpet. A whirring sound came from the wall panels.

"Come, sit." Shouma showed them comfortable seats facing each other at the center.

A low console rose between them from the floor, panels facing them. Beri's face appeared in one cell, Gisli's in another. It was hard to tell what sort of place they were in. Their faces glowed red against a black backdrop.

Yanda dropped onto her knees to draw close. "Beri? Where are you? Are you safe?" She added, "And...and you, Gisli?" She'd had little chance to get to know Gisli. They were on the road escaping and then, arriving in the elven forest, her time had been filled with helping the Stone draw back its fragments, and fighting off Krid's attacks on the elven world, while Gisli spent his time in the bunker with Merne and Tlalit.

Gisli, always honest, said, "We're not exactly safe."

Yanda realized their faces were drawn. "What can we do?"

Shouma put a hand on her shoulder. "Here. The screen can be adjusted. Sit back in your seat." She swiveled the monitor away from the rest and extended it on an arm, close to Yanda.

Over the top of the console, Ilan watched Yanda, glancing between her and his screen. He and Merne both had their own devices open next to them as well, on pull-out trays, holographic screens popping up as they tapped keys.

"Are we going to help you? Are you making plans with Shouma?" Yanda asked.

Ilan and Merne flicked their eyes up to Yanda and nodded.

She wanted to hug Beri. It had been much too long since she'd been with him and now he appeared vulnerable. She wanted to talk, just the two of them, to jibe him about the lover she'd heard about, to hear all that had happened to him. A tear trickled past her nose and she swiped at it, then leaned back. "I can't be much help with your planning so just carry on, and tell me what I need to do."

"See you soon, Mirror." Beri called her by the nickname he'd given her, once he realized she actually saw not only through a mirror but also through the wall behind it.

Things moved quickly after that, mind-speak interspersed with voices as screens shifted. Explanations shot by Yanda like a fast-moving fog. Beri and Gisli disappeared before the conversation ended. Ilan and Merne spoke in short, clipped sentences, finishing for each other as though they'd worked together a thousand times. Then they stopped and turned to Shouma.

"Ready?" she asked.

"Almost." Ilan typed streams of data into his device and watched several screens. "As you know, we identified the person on Alland who's orchestrated much of this, with ties to Blaz as well as to Kridenit. I've pinpointed the exact location under the school where Seiti is being held." He glanced at Yanda.

At the sound of her daughter's name, and the surety of her location, Yanda gripped the chair handles, ice and heat prickling through her.

"Beri and Gisli are making their way there. We will

have to be swift once we begin. We will plan a chain of shut-downs allowing access to her."

"Can't Merne just transport her out of there?" Yanda asked.

"Not in this case," Merne said. "She is rigged with a number of tags that will alert them if she is moved."

At this, Yanda's hand went to her mouth as she stared in alarm.

Shouma came to stand by her, hand to her shoulder. "We will easily remove them once we're there but..." She looked at Merne for further explanation.

"We need to be near her and I believe we'll have to spend a day or two becoming replicas of those closest to her there in the school," Merne said.

"I don't want to rush anything or jeopardize the operation but can we get started now?" Yanda's lips felt numb and uncooperative in her shock.

"We're as ready as we're going to get," Ilan said. "Beri and Gisli will give us new coordinates so we can end up close but not in the building. We don't want to give ourselves away. Tiklet has set up for attack, of course, but doesn't expect invasion from beneath. I have no idea how Beri and Gisli found their way there, or had the guts to go."

"Beri's a crazy investigative journalist. He probably dragged Gisli along." Yanda wanted desperately to know how long her daughter had been at this Blaz school for advanced psychic training, but she would not take time for such questions now.

"Okay, here it is." Merne tapped a set of keys, making all their screens show the same display.

"What am I looking at?" Yanda asked.

"A grid of Tiklet and the surrounding buildings.

There's a lot of information here but we just need to know the coordinates where we'll meet B&G."

"If you and Ilan know where we're going, then I'm ready to help us get there." Yanda took Shouma's hand.

Merne and Ilan shoved their devices into flat holders strapped fitting against their bodies, then took Shouma and Yanda's hands. The last screen was now an image in their minds. Yanda saw that new information continued to arrive in their minds, as if the computer itself took part in their mind-meld. She felt part robotic as information and the sensations of disappearance and reappearance across space simultaneously streamed through her.

CHAPTER

21

They stood in darkness, gripping each other's hands, the air was close, too warm, stultifying. Whirring sounds suggested the workings of machines. They were underground, Yanda was sure. *Is this it? Is my daughter close by?* It was all she could do to keep from running out any exit she could find to search for Seiti. Her sight, unable to penetrate the buildings above, raced outward. Out and out, through walls and across miles. She saw misery, torture, bloody enslavement. She heard cries of torment. Unable to stop, she continued her reach into mines and locked chambers. She sobbed, mind on the verge of breaking, her mouth open with a silent scream while her body stood frozen.

Ilan shook her arms. "Yanda. Stop."

Merne stepped to her. Yanda slowly registered tormented eyes looking back at her. In their mind-meld, she'd been showing Merne and the others everything she saw.

Shouma stepped behind her, hands pressed to her back, and started shutting down the vision.

As her sight closed off the distressing scenes, Yanda perceived the Stones helping, and someone else... That couple she thought of as her birth parents, though were they really? Or were they some other memory from earliest childhood? They constructed a tower in her mind, brick by brick, made of beautiful, warm memories. Yanda stood within it, seeing only her children, herself swimming in the seas of Terlond with the *tesu*, climbing in the elven forest with Zami, until her heartrate slowed and her breathing normalized.

⚍

Ilan longed to take Yanda into his arms and hold her close until her shaking stopped. He breathed deep, once, twice. Then he straightened his shoulders and pulled out a data device from his shoulder bag.

"We need to get our mind-registers neutralized, match some who live on this planet so we don't trigger surveillance. And Yanda, we need you to find Gisli and Beri." He stroked her hair gently, his only concession to the need to touch her with comforting hands. "Limit your sight, okay?" His lips barely lifted in a quick smile.

⚍

Yanda raised her hands to wet cheeks. Shakily, she said, "I'm sorry. I didn't mean—"

"Don't apologize," said Shouma. "We need to see

what kind of planet we're on. So much is hidden here, but you can show us the truth, painful as it is."

"I don't want—" Yanda choked on the words. She sucked in another breath, stepped out of the protective cocoon they'd built, and began a careful sweep of the basements in their vicinity.

"You have to use mostly sight. If you apply other mental abilities, you may be detected," Shouma said.

Yanda's vision moved past pipes and generators, the workings of the city. Unusual sources of energy intrigued her but she followed Shouma's instructions and kept to her sight, pushing through one wall after another.

Suddenly she detected Beri's mind-register. She quickly shielded the connection, then tapped into AI running on Ilan's dedicated server. Lightly, she matched her mind to resonances in the data, hiding her mind.

There they were, Beri and Gisli. She took in the area around them, lined with glowing monitors. Detecting the location in her data state of being, she gave it to the small group. They held each other's arms, dissolved and took shape in a similar underground room. Beri and Gisli showed no surprise as the four appeared in their space. Yanda detected the barriers that hid their minds as Beri stepped to her and wrapped his arms around her. She gripped him in a tight hug. How she'd longed to do that. They stayed that way for seconds, eyes shut. When they pulled apart, Yanda drank in the sight of her friend, hair redder than Ilan's. He studied her with fondness. The women hugged Gisli, a smallish, plum-brown man. Yanda's memory cast back to the first time she'd met him, when she'd drawn a sensor chip from his flesh. He'd been with them on their escape from Dondar, and in the forest of the elves. He had invaluable IT knowledge which had helped them fight Kridenit and his army.

"Okay," Gisli said, moving to a wall display. "We have about thirty minutes before the next tech shift begins and they come to go over the systems. In that time, I want to acquaint you with the Tiklet operation, what's in the walls, and who surrounds Seiti."

"How—?" Yanda had sworn she wouldn't ask how or why these two had involved themselves with her daughter on Blaz, but curiosity was driving her mad. Also, suspicions crept in. No, Beri would not betray her, sell her out. She studied his eyes, blue smudges under them. She shook her head. "Never mind. Keep going."

Gisli glanced at her but, all business, tapped on a keyboard. Yanda had never seen anything like it. Symbols glowed in layers in the air as he swiftly selected some. Then a screen appeared above, showing strangers moving around in rooms of sterile perfection. Walls flowed like water, colors moving.

And then she spotted Seiti. She'd know her daughter's red-black hair anywhere. It had a mind of its own. Even now, with it pulled into braids, some sprang out unruly around a face Yanda barely recognized. It had thinned, losing any trace of baby fat. She appeared old for eight, her features drawn, clearly intelligent, but almost…cold.

As though pulled by an invisible rope, Yanda stepped to the screen, nose nearly touching it, taking in every line on her daughter's face, searching for the girl she knew when she was six. Seiti appeared frighteningly like a stranger. For the first time, Yanda felt terrified to be reunited with her.

Seeming to sense her gaze, Seiti's eyes turned toward

the hidden camera. Yanda gasped and inched away, but not before she saw a frown line indent one of her daughter's brows. There was still beauty in her bright eyes. There always had been, but now there was an unnerving cast.

"You see the woman nearest her?" Gisli interrupted her examination. "She's her minder, the one we have to be most careful of. But don't fool yourself. Everyone in that room has formidable skills." As Gisli explained the nuances of what they observed, Yanda realized this was a school room, though one would not guess by the furnishings. Modules didn't resemble desks. Instead, shapes floated. It could be an aeronautics lab or any number of research facilities. Panels appeared and disappeared, reconfiguring the spaces.

Yanda watched for a while, then glanced around at Shouma, Merne, and Ilan. She knew they were testing mind-prints to decide which they might become. Ilan and Merne had their own holographic screens up, examining patterns. There were ten students in this section, all female, each with a minder, though apparently not all were present during lessons.

Beri finally spoke up. Though, as an investigative journalist he was a superb spy, he was not a tech genius like Gisli. "The best time will be at the transition, when she goes home for the night."

"She doesn't live in the school?" Yanda asked, lips barely moving. She felt dulled by the shock of her daughter's appearance, gripped by unnamed fears that crippled her energy.

"Oh, no," Gisli said without turning as his fingers continued to touch bright icons in the air. "Her domicile is in one of the elite neighborhoods, completely shielded from outside detection. In a dome that looks like any other from the outside."

"A domicile? Meaning…a home?" Yanda had assumed, if her daughter was in a school, she slept in a dorm with the other girls. She'd never imagined another home, another family. Another layer of emotions slathered itself on top of the guilt and shame she'd already helped herself to.

"A host family. Yes." Gisli took up the dialogue, seeming oblivious to the new reality that haunted Yanda. "The garage is far easier to access. Entering the school is just about impossible, though we've been able to rig undetectable, miniscule observation bots in most rooms."

"She rides in one particular *serstrop*, TS 19," Beri put in. "Knowing that, we've prepared a compartment in the interior structure of TS 19 where we can hide. We'll be miniature and invisible." He looked at Shouma and Merne.

"We can do that," Shouma said.

Gisli and Beri explained that three girls would be on the ride with Seiti, two of them dropped off before her. She would get out with her minder.

Shouma said, "Ilan can mask our mind registers, matching those in the vehicle."

"I think one of us will have to go into Seiti's mind as well," Beri said. "She's likely been strongly conditioned to resist, programmed to sympathize with her keepers." He winced an apology toward Yanda.

She shrugged and nodded, mouthing, "I know."

"I can become Seiti," Ilan said. "If that's okay with you, Yanda."

She glanced between them. Merne was incredibly adept at this. So was Ilan. It would probably not even work for her to be the one to go into her daughter's mind. Could she command her daughter's mind if there was a struggle? Slowly, she nodded.

They heard voices in the hallway. Gisli cleared away any sign that they'd been there and the group of six disappeared, appearing in the multi-level parking structure below the school. Invisible, they manifested comfortable chairs out of the air. Gisli shot up a holographic screen from a wrist device and they continued to watch the various rooms involved in the girls' schedule.

Eventually, the school day drew to a close. Varied work stations of translucent indigo and turquoise, orange and gold, dissolved into the flooring. Instructional charts disappeared. Even walls vanished, as though all had been phantasms.

Just as Beri and Gisli predicted, four girls with their minders walked toward the *serstrop*, TS 19 on the side, designed so that only specialized sensors read it. Gisli's cameras detected it easily. Chairs vanished as the six, small and invisible, minds shielded, jumped into the hidden compartment in the vehicle's inner frame.

The Tiklet group climbed aboard, settling into sumptuous seats, for this school was an elite and privileged clientele, trained for a purpose, value beyond reckoning. The girls chattered in hushed tones as their minders sat looking stoically ahead. Yanda had yet to hear a giggle, laugh or shout.

She braced herself to see the streets of Blaz. Their vehicle lifted. As they silently floated past bays of identical transport vans, Yanda saw other groups, boys and girls, similarly boarding for home. They left the shadowy interior of the parking structure, entering the low light of early evening. Expecting to see houses, or maybe sinister institutions, she saw almost comically sterile, pleasant sights—park benches with no one on them, bordered by flawless flowering bushes. As they approached an opening, she realized they'd been in a dome. Exiting, she saw nothing but domes as far as the eye could take in. They traveled on a raised plaz roadway enclosed by a clear tube. Of course. That was how all stayed hidden, invisible to curious eyes. A dome could show any scene: blue skies, storms. It could simulate parklands, city malls.

They entered the fifth dome along the monorail. This time, splendor surrounded their vehicle: opulent yards and homes with lush artificial grounds. The dome overhead was a perfect sky with clouds holographically drifting. While taking in the sights, Yanda held herself rigid, aware of voices in the van, but barely noticing the content of conversations, waiting for the moment when her group would jump into action.

Beri said into their minds, "The strawberry-haired girl will get off, then the smaller one with short dark hair."

They pulled up at a pink-walled residence. Sure enough, the tall girl with gold-red hair and striking features got out. As she turned their way, Yanda thought of a ferret. She and her stern looking minder entered a high gate.

The TS 19 wound along treelined lanes until the girl with short dark hair bounded out, energy seeming to be held at bay through sheer will. Her minder had a bit more spark. They even held hands as they walked away along a lane, then through an auto-opening gate.

Midway up a hill, they turned into a drive.

Gisli mind-explained, "They'll pass through a short tunnel, a sort of arbor entryway. That's where we make the change."

Seiti's minder stepped from the front seat, as Seiti herself got out. The woman placed a hand briefly on Seiti's shoulder to propel her forward. As they stepped into an ivy-covered archway, dotted with small lights along its interior, Yanda knew Ilan entered her daughter's mind.

Suddenly she sensed Seiti, small and invisible, in their tight compartment. A replica of her daughter walked on with the woman who was now controlled by Merne. The pair approached the house; Merne returned to the miniature, invisible group.

"How long will Seiti's replica stay...her?" Yanda asked, her daughter unconscious next to her, mind shut down by Shouma.

"'Til bedtime, I think," said Ilan. "She's basically a homunculus currently. Let's get out of here."

The seven disappeared, appearing in the entry of the *Sarsefi*.

CHAPTER

22

Ilan held the inert eight-year-old in his arms. Her red-black hair cascaded over his arm as her limp limbs, in a school uniform coverall, draped. Yanda's heart ached as she touched her daughter's hand, feather-light so as not to wake her. She longed to gather her to her.

"Thorough examination, then into the Flari," Chela said. She and Soni stood ready as Ilan laid Seiti on the cot near the healing pool. Shouma, Yanda, and Ilan went over her, searching for embedded microchips. Time was imperative, to make sure she was not detected.

Merne pressed her lower back, straightening from hunching before a monitor screen. "I'm detecting at least three areas of concern."

"That sounds right." Soni adjusted settings on the Flari for therapeutic cleansing and restoration.

Yanda helped undress Seiti from her Tiklet uniform with its insignia near her shoulder. They lowered her into heated, jade-green waters. This was a deeper shade than Yanda had seen in the pool. It had been turquoise the first time she herself had had a Flari treatment.

Shouma put her hands on Yanda's shoulders. "Do you remember how we worked with Tenali after the Stone chip was removed from his head? We traveled through his memories to find problematic areas that might control him."

"I remember," Yanda said, unlikely to ever forget. Her eyes burned with prolonged tension and emotion.

"I don't know if you want to go through that with your daughter, but it will have to be done right away. And there are—"

"I know. They've experimented."

"In the bone marrow," Chela said.

"I can target replacement therapies," Soni added.

"I think I want to wait for her to tell me," Yanda said to Shouma. "Maybe I shouldn't be part of this initial...probe."

The older woman nodded. "That might be wise."

"I may ask later, if she doesn't tell me," Yanda went on pensively, thinking aloud. She stepped to the healing pool and laid her hand on her unconscious daughter's forehead. "I love you," she whispered. "Whatever has happened, I love you." Yanda's throat constricted. She turned and walked away, out the door.

She was aware of the others' minds on the lower levels of the ship. They'd returned from Shouma's clan canyon. She longed to get to Zami, but instead turned, one floor down, and let herself into her sleeping chamber. She hadn't been alone for a long time. Flopping on the bunk, she curled into a ball and sobbed. Moments later, she heard a tap on the door. She almost yelled, "Go away." But then she read Ilan's mind, loud and clear, on the other side of the door. She'd thought she wouldn't want company, but she picked up the remote and clicked him in.

Standing just inside, Ilan studied her. She stared at him, eyes dry, without a smile. He climbed behind her on the bed and held her, arms wrapped around her, chin on her hair.

After a moment, she snuggled into him, cheek against his arm. Slowly, they began to talk.

"She may not—" he started.

"I know. I have no expectations. Months, years..." Yanda mumbled.

"But she—"

"She will. I'm not giving up." Yanda shoved hair back from her eyes. "If only I could take time back." Her throat ached.

"Can I finish a sentence?" he said gravely.

Yanda edged her face toward him.

On an elbow, he gazed down at her tear-streaked cheeks.

"Say it," she said.

He hesitated. "They had their eye on you all along. You just weren't aware. And the guardians you were placed with weren't up to the task of protecting you. In fact—well, we can get into that later. But you couldn't have stopped this from happening. I don't think you could have. You didn't have allies."

"Why would my parents not make sure I'd have allies? Why didn't anyone like Arc try to warn me, watch over us?" Yanda asked, lip trembling.

Ilan shook his head. "I don't know the whole of it. But

I will. I'm going to get to the bottom of this. And Yanda…"

Her gaze had drifted away but returned to his face, drawn by his serious tone.

"My life's mission is to keep you and your children safe." He hugged her close to him.

A faint smile tugged at her mouth. "Not your only mission, I hope."

He pressed his lips to hers; she returned the pressure, briefly, then put a hand to his face and moved away, running her eyes over his tired features.

She sighed. "Thank you. I know you'll do what you can." She pushed to sitting. "I'm going to check on Zami."

"Do you mind if I tag along?"

"No. I don't mind." She brushed his lips with her fingertips and stood.

Downstairs in the lounge, most of the passengers had gathered to hear the story of the rescue. Copious food heaped on trays weighed down low tables.

Yanda spotted Zami playing with a small boy his age and rushed to him.

"My nephew," Shouma explained as she handed Yanda a plate full of sticky, glazed Elznapian treats.

Late that night, Yanda sat by Seiti who'd been tucked into a camp bed near the Flari, still kept sedated. Holding her hand, Yanda rested her head on the slope-backed divan, gazing at her daughter. *She's here. At least she's here*, she thought.

Shouma sat by Yanda, sharing the divan. "I've gone through her memories to some extent. I couldn't do exactly what we did with Tenali. He had to participate in that. I was able to make a safety check, but it may take a long time to discover areas of behavior programming. However, Tlalit and Ilan have AI programs that can detect certain types of subliminal suggestion traps. If you're amenable, they can run those with her in a semi-sedated state."

Yanda hated that part of her wanted to eliminate any taint of the Blaz before she encountered her daughter in a waking state. The specter of being rejected loomed. She nodded. "Do what you think is best. Is there any sign that Tiklet knows she's here? That we're the ones who took her?"

Ilan pulled up a chair. "They're in a flurry. War may be coming. Seiti was being prepared as a child weapon of great value. They'll want her back. And now they know they can be penetrated, they'll want to know who's capable of that."

Shouma took Yanda's hand. "My people are strong. We all should get a few hours' sleep."

"I suppose," Yanda said. "Did Beri and Gisli get settled?"

"Oh, yeah. Actually a few have been invited into the city. Mnenu and Dele accepted an invitation. I think they're being hosted at a very fine hotel." Shouma checked Yanda's reaction, knowing she might be jealous over Mnenu. Getting a laugh from Yanda, she grinned.

Yanda glanced at Ilan. "Anyone else go into the city?" Yanda asked.

"Most wanted to stay and find out what happened, though Chin and the Jejods are probably next. They long to stretch out. We have an avian park."

At this, all three chuckled quietly, but then their eyes

turned back to Seiti. Her still, unconscious appearance tore at Yanda's heart.

"How long is it safe to keep her in this state?"

"As soon as she wakes, there's more chance of her mind being read remotely, or being controlled from afar," Shouma said. "That's why we want to make sure—"

"I understand," Yanda said, torn almost to breaking by wanting to look into her daughter's eyes, and preferring to hold off until she knew she was her little girl again. What kind of weapon had she been trained to be?

"We'll get to the next step in the process in a few hours," Ilan said. "Can you try to sleep?"

"I'll stay here," Yanda said.

Ilan and Shouma left, Ilan leaving reluctant backward glances. Yanda stretched out on the curving divan, trying to get comfortable. All the proper camp beds were occupied. Struggling to sleep in the low light of the spa room, she couldn't stop her mind from circling back to the Blaz. She tried to imagine them and found herself visualizing monsters. Who else could be so cruel? Was this true, though? Greed twists humans. But what could make someone turn a child into a weapon? How could they be like her and do that? She gazed at her daughter, then tried to close her eyes.

I need to talk to Ilan. Maybe he knows more. Knowing facts might help me not dehumanize them, deal with this logically. The monster-approach became a mire of emotional gunk, putting misdirected terror in her heart. She tapped on Ilan's mind. "You sleeping yet?" she asked.

"Heck no," he responded immediately.

"I'm sinking into a terrified mass of horror over the Blaz and what they might do. I was thinking maybe I should learn more about the planet, and that would ease my terrors, or at least move me from the state I'm in."

"I don't know if I can help. But want me to come up there?" He sounded eager.

"There's not much room on this divan," she said, sitting up, looking around for any spare cots and seeing none.

"I don't care," he said.

She detected his mental shrug and chuckled. She could tell he was already on the move.

"But Beri and Gisli probably know more about Blaz now," he said, climbing the stairs toward the spa room. Arriving, he crossed to her and knelt by the couch. For a moment, he studied Seiti, her small chest rising and falling, showing she still lived.

Yanda pressed her chin on a fist, also examining her daughter's inert figure. "Made into a weapon," she seethed in a whisper.

Tlalit's voice entered their minds. "Krid is one of the highest bidders for her. She wouldn't have been there much longer if you hadn't snatched her."

Horror came in waves, threatening to obliterate Yanda's sanity.

Ilan reached out and rubbed her shoulder. "You're thinking of the Blaz and Krid as insane irrational beings. They can't be confronted or even contemplated when you're thinking that way. There are elements that make up each part of them. Jealousy over powers, craving more power themselves, fear over powers they don't have, can't predict. They suspect others are worse than them. Greed is a symptom of power and fear."

"Do you think so?" she murmured, trying to take in how this might help her parse out the ability to fight them.

"Yeah, I do," Ilan answered. He pushed back her hair to see her eyes. Whatever he saw there must have prompted him to say, "You're not alone. We're going to work this out."

A face came into Yanda's thoughts, staring directly at her, very close. "Yandawi."

"Are you my mother?" Yanda asked in mind-speak, pressing her mouth to her fist, hoping the woman wouldn't grow vague or disappear.

"I am Dal'an, your birth mother. This is Ebri, your birth father." The woman pulled a man into view.

Yanda studied their unique chiseled features, detecting no warmth. They seemed tall and very thin but she had no frame of reference to tell height. "Why do you only speak to me clearly now?" she asked, fighting tears.

"We are safer communicating when you are with the Sonda, on their planet." Dal'an's eyes drifted away, then back. "You are with our granddaughter, Seitawi. It is well done."

"Where are you?" Yanda asked.

"You must work with the Stones to save us, Daughter. Please." Her parents grew dim as they had before. And then they were gone.

Ilan scooted closer to Yanda. "You need to try to sleep. Maybe you should get something from Soni, or Chela, to help. Go down to your bunk. This isn't comfortable enough."

Yanda thought of her shared room, where Vatu snuggled Zami.

"Or come to my room," he suggested, brows raised.

Tempted, she looked back at Seiti. "I can't leave her."

"You'll be more helpful if you get sleep," he pushed.

She pressed a hand to his stubbled cheek. "I don't think I could fall asleep anyway."

Soni approached them, eyes weary. "We should get her back into the Flari. I can do another flush of organs and reintroduce the blood and bone marrow revitalizers. I don't think working with her mind will be effective until that's complete."

Chela and Shouma got up from camp beds, apparently having heard some of what Soni said.

"I'll set her in," Ilan offered, unfolding his limbs to stand.

Chin hovered just inside the door. The large warrior woman came over to stand by Shouma. "I should have helped, on Blaz," Yanda heard her mutter to the older woman.

"You're the last one who should be on that planet," Shouma said, patting her face.

"It's my planet. I know it better than...most."

"And we both know why you can't be there." Shouma gave her a steady gaze.

Yanda followed Ilan to the tall-sided healing pool, with its many fixtures along inner walls, and watched as her daughter was lowered into now cerulean waters. Soni attached tubes to the girl's slender arms. A netted hammock held her below the surface. "I'm going to lower her head under," she said to Yanda as worked a mask over Seiti's head, attached to oxygen.

Yanda reached over the edge and touched the waters that glowed from beneath. She let her sight drift into her daughter, past flesh, into the cells, following the drip system in the tubes.

Shouma came to her side and put an arm around her.

"It can't hurt if I watch, can it?" Yanda asked.

"No, it won't harm the process. In fact, we can help." Shouma joined Yanda's mind as her vision traveled through Seiti, gaining understanding of what she was seeing from Yanda's surgeon expertise.

Soni briefly joined them to show the areas of concern and share what she read on her monitors. "We must remove these." She explained to Yanda, and she directed where to maneuver their sight. Yanda thought she detected admiration as she brought their vision microscopically to the smallest embedded chips she'd ever encountered. Seeing them, Yanda immediately called Chela over.

Together, they worked the invasive sensors from Seiti's flesh. Merne, who'd joined them, plucked the miniscule dampers with tweezers, inserting them onto plaz foam in in a small case, explaining, "I'll keep them in an impenetrable vault."

"That's good," Ilan said to her retreating back. "We need to study them."

"I hope we got them out before they were tracked," Yanda said, frowning.

"We've had a shield around her since we brought her on board this ship," Shouma said.

Yanda nodded, hoping that had been enough.

CHAPTER

23

S oni showed them what she detected in organs and bones. "When she first arrived, she had these levels." She pointed to them on screens. "There are controlling serums and ones that change development, of muscles, mind... I've reduced them all by half and soon I'll have extracted all, one hundred percent, I'm sure."

Yanda gazed at Soni whose slender figure resembled a young teen. Such brilliance for one who appeared adolescent, she thought. But, with talents, looks can be especially deceiving. "Are you sure?" she asked.

Glancing up from reading instrument dials, Soni nodded, assuring her, "I am. And we'll be able to check. We'll keep monitoring."

"You'll know if you've caught them all?" Yanda had to ask. "What if there's something you're not detecting?"

Ilan, hovering nearby, said, "I'll show you. I'm following all of Soni's data in my programs."

"When she's clear, we'll begin," Shouma said, squeezing Yanda's arm.

Yanda gasped as Seiti's head popped out of the water, eyes open. Smiling, she reached for Yanda.

"Not quite done," Soni said as she gently restrained Seiti's arm. "But soon."

A sob choked Yanda, and then she was climbing the steps, leaning over the side to run her hand along her daughter's face. "Seiti," she whispered.

"Mama," her daughter mouthed, tears welling.

Yanda took her hand. She brought it up as far as tubes allowed and kissed her fingers.

Alarms sounded around the ship, harsh and grating, like something wounded.

Tlalit's voice came over the speaker. "We're under attack. Increased shields are going up around the spa and control rooms. Everyone, group in one or the other. The rest is off limits. Immediately."

Yanda had never heard the tangerine-peaked elf sound so commanding but she handled it calmly in the way she did everything. Shouma stepped away from Yanda and spoke into a wrist device, probably to her people, the Sonda, about the emergency.

Tlalit woke a large holographic screen Yanda had never seen before, covering a third of one spa-room wall. It showed all parts of the ship's interior in a grid.

Beri and Gisli arrived in the spa room, rubbing sleepy eyes. The blare of the alarm continued as Gisli set up a holographic screen that could zero in on specific areas using *Sarsefi* cameras. Ilan did the same.

"Can we let Mnenu and Dele in?" Shouma asked. "They're being escorted back here from the hotel. Probably so the city's not a target. Our Sonda guard will have a watch on the doors."

"Better bring him in your way, Shouma," Tlalit said. "I'm not opening."

Moments later, Yanda saw Mnenu and Dele on a monitor, entering the control room.

From the Flari corner, Soni announced, "The revitalization is complete." She removed the drips from Seiti's arms.

Yanda bent over the tub side, not caring if she got soaked as she lifted her girl from the medicated waters.

"Hang on," Tlalit called out. To Mnenu, she said, "Take the controls," as she raced out of the room. A moment later, they heard the freight elevator open on their floor. Tlalit shoved a rolling, transparent box made of thick plaz through a cargo opening large enough to hold at least three people—if they weren't Ilan or Chin. There were air vents at intervals, and lines along the glass that must be wiring. AI can run through there, Yanda thought.

"She can't be isolated now, after all—" Yanda cried out in protest.

"Not isolated. There's room for you." Tlalit gathered pillows, blankets, and pads and dumped them into the cube.

Others, seeing her intent, hurried to help. They made a nest in the box.

"In you go," Tlalit gestured to Yanda who carried Seiti in her arms. She was so light. Despite her objections, she wasn't sure if Tlalit was trying to protect Seiti or just keep her off the radar. She capitulated and climbed the few steps into the cube.

Shouma followed her in.

Ilan watched, uneasy, and paced outside the tall, clear-plaz compartment.

"This is the best that exists for hiding all mind registers, body imprints and so on," Tlalit claimed, holding the door ajar. "I assembled it before you guys returned."

"But if we're under attack, they already know she's here. And who took her." Yanda knelt and settled Seiti on the pads, hoping they wouldn't need to make her unconscious again.

"Or they suspect. I got warnings," Tlalit explained. "They're outside Elznap's atmosphere."

"Maybe they have ships in other places as well." Ilan seated himself on a stool near the cube and used a tray as a makeshift desk. Devices out, he started madly tapping keys.

"You're right, Ilan." Gisli had made himself a compact headquarters in the corner behind the Flari, near the recovery cots. His fingers flew over the lit-up keys of his virtual board. "They're also near Terlond, Alland, and Qontaq."

Gisli and Ilan are going to have a techy love thing for sure, Yanda thought, peering out at them, holding her daughter against her.

"And Erzon!" Tik was on her own device, perched on a scaffold high on the wall.

"The Blaz have followed the entire history of the *Sarsefi*," Tlalit muttered. "I thought we'd obscured that." She headed for the door. "I'll be at the controls." She left, shoulders slumped.

"How are you?" Yanda asked Seiti as she pulled a quilt over her.

Vatu carried Zami in, Zamani behind them. Seeing Yanda, Seiti, and Shouma inside the tall, clear cube, she lifted Zami to look through the wall. Yanda blew him a kiss. "We have to be in here for a bit."

Zami stared at the sister. Yanda saw the curiosity in his eyes. They'd worked to find her, for much of his life.

Chela and Bonden brought snacks. Cots were being re-organized on either side of the pool to make more livable spaces, since they all needed to be in the protected area. Some sat or lay on cushions on the floor.

Mnenu bounded through the doorway and leapt into the long, narrow lap pool that stretched down the center of the room. He'd probably missed the waters replicated to his native ocean on Terlond. Settling Zami in Chela's lap, Vatu joined Mnenu in the salty water. Dele stretched long legs on a settee and pulled out her *zsun-zsun*. She played soft, fluting melodies that always calmed charged atmospheres.

Shouma arranged pillows against one wall inside the cube and gently encouraged Seiti's head onto her lap. Seiti complied, gazing up at her.

"I'm Shouma. I've known your mother the past couple of years, since she first left your planet." She brushed strands of Seiti's red-black hair out of her eyes.

"Shouma's a great healer." Yanda scooted close, leg against her daughter's side. "She's taught me a lot. She helped check you over for anything that might harm you."

"Have you gotten it all out?" Seiti spoke for the first time. She sounded a tad husky for an eight-year-old, strong, serious.

Yanda hadn't known what to expect, how her daughter would feel about their procedures to clear her. She felt relief like a pressure field lifting, letting in fresh air. "I-I was afraid you might not want anything removed," Yanda said in a choked voice.

"I might not have. Before."

Yanda marveled at her daughter's directness. Seiti had been a playful, silly six-year-old the last she'd seen her. Now she spoke in reasoned tones. "I feel their pull," Seiti said. "Something is still influencing me."

"Do you think they can hear you?" Yanda asked. "Can you tell?"

Shouma inserted herself. "Let's check. Seiti, will you let us go back through your memories and see if anything is left of the school's influence?"

"Okay." Seiti took her mother's hand. "Should I close my eyes?"

"It might be easiest," Shouma said gently. She glanced at Yanda, sharing profound gratitude that things were going this way.

The two women began a journey through Seiti's thoughts, starting from the most recent, when she'd left the school with them. Each set of memories stepped back further in Seiti's unconscious mind. Shouma hurried through mundane activities. The sorting happened naturally, gravitating toward moments of high emotion.

It was difficult for Yanda to watch as they observed Seiti's abduction and then procedures that were now only in her daughter's unconscious mind. Visiting them would help both of them heal, yet Yanda would never be the same knowing all the details. Shouma moved on. When invasive moments raised flags, Yanda went into those parts of Seiti's body with her sight. Shouma checked related brain activity until they had covered all the time back to when the Blaz first brought Seiti to their planet.

"She really was in Blenin, on Shagall, where Tlalit and

Merne picked up the monitor image," Yanda murmured, her stomach roiling.

"There's one place left," Shouma said.

"Stomach, near the groin?" Yanda asked.

Shouma nodded. "Almost like an ongoing bruising."

"Soni needs to zero in there soon." Yanda chewed a cuticle. "After a bit, though." She leaned close to Seiti's face. "Hey, kiddo," she whispered. "You must be starving."

Seiti's brown-amber eyes opened. "I am," she whispered, corners of her mouth trembling.

"Let's get you fed." Yanda gathered her in her arms, breathing her in. She remembered her nakedness, under the blanket, and sent a mind-call to Vatu who was still in the pool. "Do you have anything small enough for my daughter to wear?"

"I sure do." Vatu shot out of the pool, drawing gasps from passengers seated around the room as she landed nimbly on her webby feet. She fluffed out her sea-worthy outfit, which immediately dried as she strode toward the cube, drawing more sounds of admiration. She grinned through to Yanda. "Be right back."

"Footwear please," Tlalit said over a monitor as Vatu approached the door.

Seiti gazed from her mother out to the departing blue creature with mauve head nubs. Then her eyes traveled further, to the Jejods, crouching on the scaffolding that had become permanent, though it was on board mainly for repairs.

Vatu held a rubbery foot toward the monitor and wiggled her toes. "Feet protected." Tlalit laughed. "Go ahead. My mistake."

Vatu saluted toward the speaker and left to get clothing.

Tlalit announced, "The entire spa room is sealed off from detection, thanks to Ilan's AI work throughout the walls and flooring. You can come out of the cube."

As the three climbed out, Soni hurried over. "I could get Seiti back into the Flari to pinpoint that last area of concern." She looked from Yanda to Shouma for confirmation.

Seiti stood, wrapped in a silvery thermal blanket, studying the denizens of the pool room.

CHAPTER

24

An hour later, Yanda couldn't take her eyes off her daughter, face bright and animated talking to her little brother. She was dressed in Vatu's mauve and lavender one-piece outfit that a girl her age might design in a fashion notebook. They sat on the curving divan near the recovery cots, nibbling at mushroom casserole and dipping flat breads in sauces.

Zami sat cross-legged next to her, Tuk-Tuk on his shoulder, talking a mile a minute.

Ilan pulled a folding chair next to Yanda and they watched the kids get acquainted, though Ilan glanced frequently at his holographic screen.

Mnenu, Zamani, Beri, and Gisli came from the control room. The whole ship had now been pronounced safe. The new group circled chairs around them, screens up, discussing Blaz sightings.

Seiti's mind seemed clear and untainted, though Yanda

wanted Ilan to run his AI programs through every bit of her. She jumped as a familiar voice called in her mind. Was it only for her? She looked around. No one else seemed to hear Tenali. He said to her, "Okay, the Stones won't leave me alone now that I'm back in Known Space."

"You went into Unknown Space?" Yanda asked, heart speeding up. "Are you okay?"

"Yeah. Lots to tell. But we need to get you onto Ter-lond to do what you did with the fragments."

"I know. This time with a whole moon. But maybe you aren't aware the Blaz are staked out all over the universe— well, at all the planets we've recently been to."

"You found your daughter, though. You've got her?"

"Yes. I can't believe you didn't know that."

"Mom and I haven't had a lot of chance to chat lately. And as I said—"

"You just got back into livable space," she finished for him.

Ilan looked at her strangely.

"Sorry, it's…" She tapped her temple.

"Tuh-nolly?" Ilan tried the name he'd heard her think.

"Stop listening." She swatted his leg.

Tenali asked, in her head, "Who's the big red-haired fellow?"

Reticent, Yanda brought both men into her mind. "Tenali, meet Ilan. Ilan, Tenali."

In her mind, they could see each other as she saw them. She certainly didn't want to share her entire history of one with the other. Soon her head ached from choosing what memories to hide so she closed them both out again. Individually, she said to Tenali, "I'm going to head down to my bunk and we can talk a bit." To Ilan, she said, "I'll explain later. For now, I have to find out if there's something urgent I need to do. Apparently, the Stones helped him enter Unknown Space, and now are exacting payment. Sort of. Though maybe what they want is good for all of us." She stood to leave.

Ilan took her hand and pulled her so he could speak in her ear. "That's fine. Go talk to Tenali. But I know that what the Stones are demanding has to do with your parents, and I'm not sure..." He hesitated, then blurted, "I'm not sure it's good, Yanda." He seemed to hate saying it.

She straightened and studied him, disbelief raging in her, unwillingness to countenance this possibility quite at this moment. The Elves appeared to worship the Xentu part of her. Everyone did.

"Remember the foul black vapor we drew out of Bonden?" he went on. "It has something to do with them. You know it does."

She shook her hand loose from his and, taking deep steadying breaths, walked away.

~ THE END ~
Stay tuned for Book 4

MISSING MOON GLOSSARY

Akrat (ah-KROT): swear word in Qontaqian.

Aktat (ahk-TAHT'): bird-like Jejod, oldest of the three sisters.

Alland (ah-LAHND): terra-formed planet where Yanda grew up; no trees, no oceans, no hills.

Arc: man of strong mind powers; centuries-old; keeper of Pedore.

Ash-don (ASH-dawn): Power stone of the Neyla, Shalt's equivalent.

Balyou (BAL-you): Yanda's home town on Alland.

Belsom (BEL-sum'): Qontaqian moon.

Beri (BEH-ree): captive of Krid, journalist from Romden; Yanda's friend.

Blaz (blahz): planet known for trafficking, torture, slavery.

Blenin (BLEH-nin): city on Shagal, where Seiti may have been spotted.

Bonden (BON-din): Qontaqian; one of the ten fems held in captivity by Krid; inventor, strong powers, can walk through walls.

bonga beans: popular with only a few, found in out-of-the-way places in the universe.

Brend Alley: popular part of Prokit's Moon. AI mecca connecting the universe.

cabreeli: venal character of Qontaq.

chaka: like hot chocolate.

Chela (CHEH-lah): healer, fellow captive of Krid.

Chin (Chinkendit): large soldier, mind powers, fellow fem captive.

chochoi: Sonda endearment.

Cillen (sih-LEN): powerful woman who seems to run Pedore, Keeper.

cratat (kruh-TAUT): mean's cool in Rotoulian (wood elves)

Da-Lam (duh-LAHM): program with powerful AI, allows encrypted searches, combines with mind powers for some.

Dal'an (DAH-LAHN): Yanda's Xentu mother.

Decru (*deh-KROO*): silver-haired Neyna elf elder; mainly occupies the underground labyrinth in Shalt's caves.

Deladar (deh-la-DAR): Jejod city on Erzon.

Dondar (dawn-DAHR): main city on Terlond's single continent.

dravis (DRA-vis): wood elf expression, like good grief or heavens.

Ebri (EH-bree): Yanda's Xentu father.

Elznap (ELZ-nap): Shouma's home planet.

ENAC 370: high-level portable computer.

Enders: café in Deladar on Erzon.

Erzon (ehr-ZAHN): Jejods' planet; part cloud mass.

fems: females of humanoid species

Flari (FLAW-ree): regeneration tub designed Soni in the underground refuge, Pedore, on Alland.

Gisli ("GIZ-lee"): from a small threatened planet; purplish-brown skin. Highly trained in military IT.

Glaus (GLOSS): Sonda city on Elznap.

holo-screen: holographic computer monitor.

hopo (HOH-poh): vehicle on Prok, magnetic field carries them along without fuel.

Ilan (ih-LAUN): big red-haired man from Qontaq; can shield powerfully. Was part of the Alland underground when he and Yanda met.

Jat (JAHT): middle Jejod sister.

jeloli: native flower of Prokit's Moon with cleansing properties.

jhal tree: On Erzon

Jejod (juh-JOD): bird-like humanoids; warrior sisters: Aktat, Jat, Tik.

Jelat (jel-LAUT): Keepers of Pedore, often in the city of Skarth on Alland; tech whiz, betrayed Yanda.

kaffe **(KAF):** coffee-like Terlondian drink.

kari berries: of Erzon

koddler: vehicle for land and air on Erzon.

Kridenit "Krid": evil mage; collects objects and creatures with powers.

Lalut (lah-LOOT): prism-shaped electronic device.

Lantat (lawn-TAUT): town on Belsom.

lanten (LAN-tin): form sea Elves can take, as sea creature.

La'prel (luh-PREL): Shouma's family dynasty.

Lark: Tenali's ship.

Lilanca (lih-LAHN-kuh): Tedro's medical ship

Merne (murn): Neyna forest elf leader, Zamani's daughter, hair brown and green; can transform herself into other appearances. Tenali is her only son.

Mingal (ming-GAHL): a far planet at the edge of the known universe, all ocean.

Mnenu (mNAY-noo): male sea elf; leader of Ash-don's powerful Circle of minds.

Neyla (NAY-luh): sea elves on planet Terlond.

Neyna (NAY-nuh): wood elves of Terlond.

Pedore (peh-DOR-eh): secret underground refuge for talents on Alland.

Phanic: guard on Qantoq.

plaz: synthetic material made from recyclables or plant fibers; can be thin as paper or thick enough for furniture.

plunka-toys: plaz pieces that fit together to build elaborate structures.

Prokit's Moon (PRAH-kit) (or "Prok"): orbits Erzon; favorite destination for artist, writers, musicians, all arts, techies.

Qontaq (kon-TAHK): planet with conflict between those who have powers and those who don't.

Ralashal (*rah-lah-SHAHL*): a Neyla game played with small painted shells.

Rotoul (roh-TOOL): elven forest on Terlond.

Sandu (sahn-DOO): planet with large freighter business.

Sarsefi (sahr-SEH-fee): Tlalit's ship; name. means love-making.

Seiti (SAY-tee): Yanda's daughter, missing.

serstrop (SEHR-strop): passenger van on Blaz; runs on rails.

SG: Senden Geres. Military research facility on Qontaq.

Shagal: moon where Seiti might have been caught on camera monitor.

Shalt: immense power stone of the Neyna.

Shamba's Nook: café on Belsom.

sharran floss: soft fiber from the jhal tree on Erzon, used by the Jejods.

Shouma (SHOO-muh): woman with formidable mind powers, captive with Yanda, trained the fems' mind powers; of the Sonda people.

Shagall (sha-GAWL): moon in Alland's star system.

Sinisay ("SIN-i-ssay"): that part of the government that monitored talent, prevented its use, sequestered its powers.

Skarth: main city on Alland, where Yanda was surgeon; large spaceport.

Sonda (SAWN-duh): Shouma's people.

sondo: Neyla word, a minute.

Soni (SOH-nee): a Keeper of Pedore; Healer, inventor.

swizzer (SWIZ-zer): a sled that floats using a magnetic field, used especially in caves.

Tedro (TED-roh): Shouma's son; merchant; has medical supply ships.

Tenali (ten-NAW-lee): half-elf son of Merne, grandson of Neyna leader, Zamani

Terlond (tehr-LAWND): planet of Yanda's captivity; where the woodland and sea elves live. Mostly ocean.

Tik ("teek"): youngest Jejod sister.

Tiklet (tih-KLET): sinister training school on Blaz.

Tlalit (TLAH-lit): female wood elf; tangerine peaked hair; Merne's lover, captain of the Sarsefi.

Tuk-tuk (TOOK-took): tiny primate native to Terlond.

Unknown Space: dark matter is different, hurts ship engines; little exploration there, no settlements.

Vatu (VAH-too): fellow fugitive on Terlond; home planet Mingal; can transform.

wakneet vine: flowering scented vine growing on Alland.

Wayfarer: inn where they stayed on Belsom.

Withum (WITH-um): flower whose pollen brings on a great mind-meld among the elves and others with mind powers one day a year.

Xentu (ZEN-too): powerful, long-living people who have been missing from the Known Universe for some time.

Yanda (YAWN-duh): main character; was a surgeon on Alland. Yandawi: Yanda's Xentu name

Zamani (zah-MAH-nee): leader of the forest elves on Terlond.

Zami (ZAH-mee): Yanda and Zamani's half-elf son.

zhoun-zhoun (ZOON-zoon): flute-like instrument of Qontaq.

Zotoul (zo-TOOL): Neyla realm, including reefs and waters.

LIST OF ALL THE PLANETS GROUPED IN STAR SYSTEMS

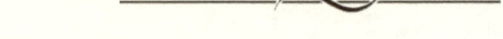

Star system: Berson Sector

Alland: (Yanda's home planet)

Shagal: (moon with wild trader city Blenin where Seiti was spotted)

Star system: Aband Sector

Terlond: Elves, captivity

Mir: [Farn is one of its four moons]

Star system: Craspel Sector

Romden: (Beri)

Tellot: planet of fragile, semi-tropical climate and nonviolent culture.

Dorn: planet known for high quality, innovative tech, often elegant in style.

Star system: Sentori Sector

Blaz: planet of traffickers, forced labor, mining and torture

Elznap (Shouma, of the Sonda culture)

Ontil (waterworld with unique sea creatures, many intelligent, such as Takmik)

Star system: Merdon Sector

Qontaq: (Bonden, Dele, Ilan)

Belsom: moon of Qontaq, city Lantat

Sandu: planet with large freighter system; Shouma's son and grandchildren

Erzon (planet of the Jejod; has Prokit's Moon)

Star system: Telori Sector

Mingal: sea world, Vatu's home

Marie Judson is an avid fantasy and sci-fi reader. She's been an editor, coffee roaster, and college professor. She lives on the wild coast of Northern California.

Visit her blog and sign up for her newsletter:

www.mariejudson.com